Thick coils slithered in the silence under the sea. Two eyes swivelled, searching for prey. A pulse of white light stabbed the inky water and mighty jaws gaped wide as one more victim sank towards the waiting rows of teeth.

Meanwhile, in another part of the ocean, a strange, dome-shaped machine scuttled over the ocean floor on retractable crab legs. Two yellow searchlights scanned the depths. At the controls, a man hummed quietly to himself. "Good fishy," he whispered. "Come to Daddy, then."

Also by Henrietta Branford

Spacebaby
Dimanche Diller
Dimanche Diller in Danger
Dimanche Diller at Sea
(*also available on audio cassette*)

Ruby Red
Hansel and Gretel
Royalblunder
Royalblunder and the Haunted House

For older readers

The Fated Sky
Chance of Safety
Fire, Bed and Bone
(*also available on audio cassette*)
White Wolf

Picture books for younger children

Birdo
Someone, Somewhere

HENRIETTA BRANFORD
Illustrated by Ellis Nadler

Collins
An imprint of HarperCollins*Publishers*

For the Monster of Loch Ness,
May she be happy ever after

First published in Great Britain by Collins in hardback in 1999
First published in paperback by Collins in 2000
Collins is an imprint of HarperCollins*Publishers* Ltd,
77-85 Fulham Palace Road, Hammersmith, London W6 8JB

The HarperCollins website address is
www.**fireandwater**.com

3 5 7 9 10 8 6 4

ISBN 0 00 675457 0

Printed and bound in Great Britain by
Omnia Books Limited, Glasgow
Glasgow G64

CONTENTS

1 Splashdown!

I woke to find water all around me. Lots of it, all going up and down. I wasn't worried – I'd programmed my craft to splash down in the sea. A robot arm lifted me carefully from the mother ship and set my silver sea pod gently down on the water. The arm paused and stuck its thumb up before telescoping back into the mother ship with a friendly wave. I lay back and watched the lovely colours fill the sky.

When I sat up, everything rocked. I lay back down and a small bare foot hovered in the air in front of my nose. Another one appeared. They waved to me and wiggled ten tiny toes. I made a grab for them and found that they were mine. That's when I knew that I'd done it again. I should have been sixteen years old, tall and good-looking. Instead I was lying flat on my back wearing nothing but a life jacket, bouncing like a pea on a drum with every passing wave.

I went back over all my sums, using toes as well as fingers. It wasn't easy, with only ten of each. Where I come from, we have enough to do really long sums. Earth creatures, who only have ten fingers and ten toes, can't manage anything more complex than the decimal system. Hector can't even manage that. I'll tell you about Hector later.

It didn't take me long to work out where I'd gone wrong. I'd done my sums correctly – except for one small but significant detail. I was sixteen all right: sixteen months, not sixteen years. How could I have been so careless? I shut my eyes and cried myself to sleep.

When I woke up, the sea was going up and down a lot more than before. A wave slapped at my pod, bouncing me up into the air. I hung there for a long moment, then belly-flopped back. I found that I was lying in a puddle. Luckily it was still warm but I could tell that pretty soon I'd be uncomfortably chilly. I felt seasick and bewildered.

By and by the wind died and the sea grew flat and sparkly. Big white birds swooped overhead, shouting things about fish: "*Nice bit of pilchard on the port bow. Herring coming up astern*!" I could hear music, too. I rolled over and got into my crawling position and from there I sat up carefully: I was already getting my sea legs – or to be more accurate, my sea bottom. I rolled a bit and slid about but I managed to stay upright.

I could see a sandy beach and a seaside fairground with swing-boats and a merry-go-round. There was a brass band playing and there were babies everywhere: babies in sun hats and babies in swimsuits and quite a few babies in birthday suits. Most of them were eating ice cream dipped in sand. It looked very tasty. Down among the waves, the bigger children splashed and shouted.

All of a sudden I felt a kind of tingle coming up through the pod. I felt it in my bottom first, because I was sitting down. Then it shot up my arms and all down my legs. It buzzed all over me. I haven't got much hair but what I have got stood on end. I knew at once that this peculiar feeling was a mild electric shock. It only lasted for a few seconds and my pod protected me from the worst of it. Something much worse was happening to the children who were playing in the sea.

Every single one of them let out a shriek.

Sparks flew out of their noses. Their hair stood on end and crackled. Those with straight hair suddenly had curls. Those with curls had frizz. They shot out of the water, dashed up the beach and clung to their mothers or their fathers or their best friends – or even to people they didn't much

like, if nobody else was at hand. They stood, mouths open, eyes round, hair on end, pointing back at the sea. The merry-go-round slowed to a halt. The brass band stopped playing. Behind the beach, the little seaside town filled with the sound of crumpling metal and rude words as traffic lights failed and cars slid into other cars.

Time to talk to Tipperary, I decided. I reached for my mobile phone. It was completely dead. I had my microcomputer with me, tucked into my nappy – I don't go anywhere without it – but it was dead, too. That was when I began to get scared.

You might be wondering why I had returned to Earth. After all, things didn't go exactly smoothly last time I was here. Well, Tipperary had left a message I just couldn't ignore on my intergalactic website and that's what brought me back. The message said: *Urgent! Strange things happening at sea. Please come immediately.*

I wrote my mum and dad a note: Gone to Earth, Back Friday. Which means: *Gone to Earth. Back Friday*. And here I am.

Meanwhile my pod was going round in circles like a wind-up toy. Close ahead of me, a line of jagged rocks stuck up through the waves like teeth. Each circle of my pod was carrying me nearer to those sharp stone spikes. I left the beach behind and soon a wild-looking headland appeared. Heather grew between tumbled shoulders of rock. Stunted trees with strange haircuts the wind had given them twisted back from the sea.

I didn't want to be swept out to sea – and that can happen easily in a lightweight pod. But neither did I want to prang my little pod on those pointed pinnacles. If I did that, it would burst like a balloon.

In the end, it wasn't the rocks that sank me but a tangled mixture of flotsam and jetsam – chunks of polystyrene, plastic drink bottles and part of an old wooden crate, all wound up in some orange netting and tied together with nylon fishing line. Several big sharp hooks were knotted into the line. They snagged my pod, there was a sudden hiss and I found myself bobbing up and down in the freezing cold water. I pulled my knees up to my chin and began to yell.

I had managed two good hollers when I heard a really tremendous **whooooshhshs!!!** like a rocket going off just behind my head. I opened my eyes. It *was* a rocket going off behind my head. I had programmed it to fire on contact with water, just in case. It hurtled up into the sky, calling for help to anyone who might be watching. It's lucky for me that someone was, or this story would be a whole lot shorter.

I must have swallowed litres of sea water but there was plenty left to slap my face, sting my eyes, rush up my nose and swirl round inside my ears. The power of the sea is absolutely tremendous. You'd never know it, just to look at them, but quite ordinary waves could toss an elephant into the air, or tug a rhinoceros under. And I was just a tiny, floating baby.

All of a sudden, an unforgettable smell of wet dog hit me right on the nose. You might think that wet dogs smell the same on any planet, but I would have known this one anywhere. Happiness filled my heart. There, dog-paddling valiantly towards me through the crashing waves, his round brown eyes gleaming a welcome, his floppy ears flying and his little stumpy tail wagging joyfully, was my old friend, Hector! He had seen the distress rocket and, with no thought for his own safety, leapt to the rescue.

We didn't waste our breath on any *Hi-there-bro* business, I can tell you. Hector grabbed me by the back of my life jacket, swung us both around and headed for the shore. We were in deadly danger of being swept straight back out to sea by the undertow, and Hector needed all his strength to fight the boiling, moiling waves. We were both near to exhaustion by the time we saw Tipperary, lying on her surf board, paddling towards us for all she was worth. She ploughed up alongside us and with one scoop of her arm she hoisted Hector and me on to her board. Then she stood up with me held tight in her arms, flipped the board around and caught the crest of the wave for the long ride back to shore.

Hector's ears flew back in the wind and he yipped with excitement. It was a fantastic feeling, balancing between sea and sky, swooping and dipping, turning and twisting, with the white surf bubbling like champagne all round us and the salt wind buffeting our faces as we powered down the long roller and back on to the beach.

2 Cyberee

Soon I was safe inside **SOFTIE** – that's Tipperary's *Super-de-Luxe Family Travel Experience* – enjoying a hot power shower while Hector gently licked the sand and salt away.

SOFTIE is Tipperary's home. She built the bus herself and put in every kind of Information Technology – well, every kind they have on Earth, which frankly isn't much – as well as plenty of home comforts. There were bunk beds and a Comfy Dog-Eze basket for Hector. There was a roomy nesting and perching area for Aunt Doris's hens – Aunt Doris always brings them with her when she comes to visit because she doesn't trust anyone else to look after them properly. There was a power shower, as I've already said, and a snack bar and a stack of toys and loads of books and videos and CDs and computer games. **SOFTIE** has a powerful engine, too, and a sleek, aerodynamic chassis. That bus was a work of art and Tipperary was the artist.

Hector and I are like brothers: he gets right on my nerves and I get right on his. There are a thousand things he does that drive me crazy. He licks me. He barks in my ear. He nicks my rusks. He chews my toys. And he's *so snooty* – just because I wear a nappy and he doesn't. Worst of all, he tries to get Tipperary's attention *all* the time. He often reminds me that Tipperary belonged to him before I ever got here. He thinks that gives him special privileges but I know that Tipperary loves me just as much as she loves him. She missed me like anything when I went home. I missed her, too. I missed her big warm smile and the funny way she talks. She looks pretty funny as well. Earth people do. For a start they have only one head. It just doesn't seem enough, does it?

"But what were you *doing* in the sea, Moses?" Tipperary asked, once I was safely snuggled up beside Hector under his tartan Cozee-Boy blanket. "Why didn't you tell us you were here?"

"I was going to,Tipperary," I explained. "I came as soon as I got your message. But when I got here my phone went dead and my computer shut down."

Hector snorted, spraying me with dog dribble. "Ibetwhatever'sgoingonisallyourfaultwobblehead!" he barked. Whenever anything goes wrong, Hector thinks it's my fault. "OKbigheadtelluswhat you'vedonethistime!" he yipped. I couldn't answer immediately, because Tipperary was pulling my vest on over my head. She popped a disposable nappy on the other end and looked round for some baby clothes. As it happened, Aunt Doris had just finished knitting me a pretty cool outfit. She can't seem to remember that I'm a different shape and size back home, but for here and now, the suit she'd knitted was just right. Tipperary pulled it out of Aunt Doris's sewing basket and tried it on me. It was soft and warm and stripy – pink and purple, my favourite, with a little flap at the back for nappy changing. Tipperary buttoned me into it and sat me on her lap.

"Good job you're still the same size," she said. "Or are you? I think you're a wee bit smaller, Moses." Hector snorted again when I told her that I had slipped up with my sums, but Tipperary smiled and kissed me. "Never mind, moonshine," she said. "I think you're lovely this age. Isn't he lovely, Hector?" Hector snorted some more. "Aunt Doris is going to be so pleased to see you,

Moses," Tipperary went on, ignoring Hector and patting my little chubby cheeks. "She's here on a visit, with the hens. She's taken them out for a breath of sea air but she'll be back any minute. Look – here she comes now!"

Tipperary lifted me up so I could see out of the window, and there was Aunt Doris, stumping along the windy beach, with her hat pulled well down and her mackintosh flapping. Bess and the rest of the chickens were blowing all about her feet. Hens aren't much good at flying, as a rule, but each time the sea breeze caught them, it lifted them squawking off the ground, blew them along a little way and dropped them back down. It was a kind of chicken wind-surfing and they were loving it. Hens need a bit of adventure, just the same as everybody else. I understand hens pretty well, because of speaking chicken. And besides, Bess the Buff Orpington was a particular friend of mine.

Aunt Doris absolutely beamed when she saw me. "Well Moses!" she exclaimed. "Fancy seeing you here! Dropped in for a bit of a holiday, have you? So have we. But you look chilly dear – I hope you haven't been paddling. It's much too cold for that, my pet."

"I know," I said. "I didn't mean to, Aunt Doris."

Hector chuckled. "And I didn't come on holiday exactly, either."

"Didn't you, dear? Never mind, it's lovely to see you. I hope whatever brought you here has nothing to do with your old computer nonsense."

"Well, it might have," I said, cautiously.

Hector sat up straight and scratched his ear. **"Doneitagainnappybottom!"** he barked happily.

"Have not!" I barked back.

"Now, now," Aunt Doris soothed, taking me from Tipperary's arms and giving me a cuddle. "Just you begin at the beginning, my duck, and tell us all about it." She often calls me her duck. I don't know why.

"Well," I began. "Do you remember CYBERFLOAT?"

"**Howcouldweforgetfluffhead?**" Hector chuckled.

CYBERFLOAT is my favourite computer game. It's all about being stuck on a planet where something's gone wrong with gravity and you have to find a way to fix it before everything floats off into space. There are several different levels but the one that I like best is **Heavy Moon**, where giant electric eels are invading the galaxy. You have to ZAP them into black holes to get rid of them.

"Remember **Heavy Moon**?" I asked.

A strange look crossed Tipperary's face – a suspicious look. "Didn't it have something to do with giant electric eels, Moses?" she asked. I nodded. There was a little silence. Then Tipperary shook her head. "*You haven't, Moses,*" she whispered. "*Tell me you haven't.*"

"**Hashashas!**" barked Hector, bouncing up and down.

"Well," I said, blushing a bit. " might have. Sort of. Accidentally."

Hector grinned and helped himself to half a dozen biscuits from his personal biscuit dispenser. He knows perfectly well that he's not supposed to do that without asking, but he could see that Tipperary was concentrating too hard on me to take any notice of him. He even sneaked a quick bite out of a chocolate cake Aunt Doris had made earlier. Then he lay down on his beanbag with chocolate round his chops, looking cheerful.

Tipperary sighed and shook her head. "Do you know what's been going on here?" she asked. "Ships' compasses have gone crazy. Birds and whales and all sorts of creatures have been migrating in the wrong direction. Computers have gone berserk. Huge power surges are coming from under the water and nobody knows what's causing them. Are you trying to tell us that an electric eel off a computer game is doing all that?"

"Well, it might be..." I said.

"I'm not at all surprised," Aunt Doris interrupted. "I never did trust those computers. Nasty old things they are, buzzing away. And what good do they do, eh? They can't lay you a nice speckled egg, can they? Not like my Bess.

We were quiet for a while. Then I spoke again. "The thing is, Aunt Doris," I explained, "I'm not talking about a *cyber* eel. I'm talking about a *real* eel. From outer space."

"I wonder if they taste like worms?" Bess clucked. "Or would they be more fishy? I don't really care for fish. But I do enjoy a good plump worm."

"Here's what I think could have happened," I explained quickly – because once Bess starts talking about worms, you're liable to be there for hours and hours while she clucks on about long thin tangy ones and short fat buttery ones and chewy ones and squidgy ones and ones that wiggle inside your insides. "You remember when I zapped an eel playing **Heavy Moon**? And it zapped me back and the double zap zapped all the way to Earth and landed at the North Pole? And afterwards we zapped the North Pole with an electromagnetic surge from the Internet?" I asked.

"Coursewedoegghead," Hector snorted, helping himself stealthily to more cake.

Tipperary and Aunt Doris nodded in a grim kind of way. I could see that they remembered too.

"Well, zapping is how eels talk," I said. "Electric eels, that is. And I've got a feeling – just a feeling, mind – that the **ZAP** I zapped might possibly have called one of them down to earth. Kind of earthed it, you might say."

"But Moses," Aunt Doris croaked. "You surely don't mean to tell us that there really are giant electric eels in space? Nasty great squirmy things? Wriggling round the galaxy on the loose?"

"There might be," I replied. "Nobody knows for sure. It's been suspected for a long time. We've got all kinds of stories about giant eels at home. They used to be called Dragons. From time to time, our astronomers pick up strange pulses of energy from space – Dragon Talk, they call it. Some people believe there really are space eels out there. Some don't. I've always believed in them. And now I think there's one here, on Earth – or rather, in the sea."

"Perhaps that **ZAP** was like a kind of mating call," Tipperary murmured. "Think of it, Moses. Your dragon eel, if it exists, may have fallen in love with a cyber eel. That's kind of sad, don't you think?" Hector snuffled. Aunt Doris shook her head. Bess crept behind the tea cosy.

"I suppose it is," I nodded. "But I can't help it. I didn't mean to make it happen. Why are you all looking at me like that? It's not *my* fault. I'd like a nice bottle, if you don't mind, Tipperary. And a dry nappy. And a sleep."

"Quite right, my duck, don't you go getting all upset," Aunt Doris said, and put the milk on to warm up for my bottle.

3 Charley Cool

When I woke up, warm and safe and tucked into Tipperary's bed, I was hungry again. Babies are hungry all the time because our stomachs only hold an eggcupful of food at a time. Also, my nappy needed changing – for much the same reason. Tipperary took care of both problems. There are nice things and nasty things about being an Earth baby. Having freezing cold cream slapped on your bum is bad. Having your nappy taken off is good. But what I like best of all is sucking on a bottle of warm milk. Tipperary knew just how to feed me. She let me hold the bottle for myself and she didn't mind if I dropped it or dribbled. A lot of milk goes down your neck and round behind your ears, when you drink from a bottle – you try it, if you don't believe me. Tipperary wiped me down and found me a clean babygrow. When she had finished, I asked her if **SOFTIE**'s communication systems were working.

"Everything went dead for a while after that electric shock," she told me. "Phone, fax, radio, computers, the lot. But I've got it all back on now. Who do you want to talk to?"

Before I could reply, there was a light tap on **SOFTIE**'s door and Charley Cool came bounding in with his black braids flying. Charley's a special friend of ours. He works for *News Round* and he'd come to report on the strange events at sea. Journalism was Charley's job but his hobby – well, more than a hobby really, you could call it a passion – was hang-gliding. He had his trusty hang-gliding gear with him now, folded into a new silver backpack. Charley's other big passion was Tipperary. He was mad about her. He had been ever since he first saw her. And she was mad about him.

He did a double-take when he saw me. "Good to see you, little buddy," he smiled. "How's the ace from space?"

"Fine, thank you, Charley," I said. "How's hang-gliding?"

"Cool, man," Charley answered. "I've done some real high flying since I saw you last. Tipp's going to try it next and she thinks Hector might give it a go as well." Tipperary looked as though she couldn't wait, but Hector didn't look too keen. Somehow, I can't see Hector hang-gliding. But then, I never thought I'd see him surfing, either. "You here on a social visit?" Charley asked. Hector snorted. Aunt Doris dried me off and frowned at him.

"Now, Hector," she said. She may not speak dog, but she knew what he meant. "If Moses had anything to do with whatever's gone wrong under the sea, Moses will put it right. Won't you, my lamb?" I nodded. She calls me her lamb as well as her duck. Sometimes she calls me her little apple dumpling.

"You mean *you're* at the bottom of this?" Charley asked. "One thing I love about you, little dude – when you're around, life's never boring." I filled Charley in about **Heavy Moon** and giant electric eels from space.

"So tell me," he said, when I'd finished explaining. "What are you gonna do about this big eel?"

"I'm going to make friends with him," I said.

"Are you sure that's wise, dear?" Aunt Doris asked. "Friendship is a wonderful thing but you can't be too careful these days."

"The thing is, Aunt Doris," I explained, "I've got to find a way to send him back into space, so I have to talk to him. Do you think you could make **SOFTIE** amphibious, Tipperary?"

"Turn **SOFTIE** into a boat?" Tipperary said, thoughtfully. "Yes. I think so. In fact I'm sure I could. But it'll take me a couple of days."

"That's OK," I said. "Because I don't think the real trouble is going to start until the eel gets hungry and eels can go for ages without eating. Provided this one had a good meal before he left home, we should be fine. Eels are wonderful creatures – did you know they can come out of the water, Tipperary, and travel overland?"

Aunt Doris glanced out of the window nervously. "Tipperary," she said, "help me shut the windows. I want to keep the hens inside. Somehow I'd feel more comfortable if they were under my eye."

Aunt Doris made supper after that and we had a lovely evening. It felt good to be sharing Hector's comfy Dog-Eze basket and swapping jokes with Bess. Bess knows a lot of jokes about chickens. For eggsample:

Why did the chicken cross the road?

Because she wanted to get to the other side.

Actually, that's not very funny to me. I think chickens have a different sense of humour. I tried one of mine on Bess:

Why did the barracuda blush?

Because she found the eel shocking.

Bess didn't understand, but Hector laughed till he got hiccups and Tipperary had to burst a paper bag behind his head to get rid of them.

When it was bedtime, I begged to be allowed to sleep in Hector's basket. He snores a bit, but so what – I dribble. Me and Hector go back a long way.

Tipperary tucked us in together and we lay watching the glow from the lamp and listening to the grown-ups talking quietly. By and by, Tipperary took down her didgeridoo and played some of that deep, rich music that reminds me of home.

The last thing I saw before I closed my eyes was Charley and Tipperary sitting side by side, looking out at the moonlit sea. Tipperary leaned her head on his shoulder and his black braids mingled with

her orange ones. His arm crept round her waist; he wiped a smudge of dirt off her face and kissed her shyly on the cheek.

"There's something I want to ask you, Tipperary," he said quietly. "I've wanted to ask it a long time. Because you mean the world to me. You're my hang-gliding, Tipperary. You're my surfing. You're my sea and my sky. You're my sun, moon and stars. You're everything to me, Tip. Everything." Tipperary didn't answer. "So I guess I'll just ask you," Charley went on, after a while. "Shall I?"

A tiny snore escaped from between Tipperary's lips. Charley sighed. He tucked her up next to Aunt Doris on the fold-out bed, wriggled into his own sleeping bag and lay down on the floor close to me and Hector.

Outside, small waves fizzed and rippled on the rocks. A pair of lovers hugged and whispered on the beach. Beyond them lay the bay, like crumpled silver foil, under a shining moon. And if Charley had been looking out of the window at all that, he would have seen something else besides.

Far out to sea, something smooth and sleek and spotted like a leopard rose silently above the dark water. Small sparks flickered up and down its long, slim body. Behind it, something skull-shaped broke the surface. Two glaring yellow beams caught the sleek head in their crossbeam for a moment and then vanished, leaving only a smear of oil to show where they had been.

But Charley didn't see any of that because he wasn't looking out of the window. He was looking at Tipperary, fast asleep beside Aunt Doris. He saw me down in Hector's dog basket, still wide awake. "Good night, little buddy," he whispered. "Sleep tight. Mind the fleas don't bite."

"Haven'tgotfleas," Hector said, without opening his eyes.

4 Mayday! Mayday!

Next day, Charley hired a helicopter and set off to search for giant eels. Before he left, he turned to Tipperary. "Did you hear much of what I said last night?" he asked, blushing a bit. "Before you went to sleep?"

Tipperary shook her head. "I think I must have dropped straight off. Was it important, Charley?"

"Yes," said Charley. "Very."

"You'd better tell me again, then," Tipperary suggested.

"I will," he promised. "Soon."

Charley reported in to us at regular intervals. He told us he'd seen a long, dark spotted shape, winding through the water, but when he'd dipped down low to take a closer look, it dived. Several fishing boats reported seeing something similar. The captain of one said he had seen a sea monster with glaring yellow eyes. The news spread fast and tourists flocked in, eager for a sighting.

Tipperary worked fast to convert **SOFTIE** into a boat. Under her skilful hands the chassis changed into a hull, which she coated with rubber to protect us from electric shocks. She fixed large outriggers on each side to stabilise us, as well as inflatable water wings, and she built a rudder at the back so we could steer. Aunt Doris stocked up the galley – that's what you call a ship's kitchen – with useful items like ice cream, rusks, hen food, whisky and dog biscuits. She stitched a red canvas sail to boost the engine, and Tipperary made the roof into a deck, with boards for you to walk on without scratching the paint work, and railings to stop you falling overboard. She put up a mast to hold the sail, and Aunt Doris rigged up a clothes line.

We were just sitting down for a well-earned snack when Charley's call came over the radio. He sounded terrified. "**Mayday! Mayday!**" he hollered. "*My compass is spinning like a top, I don't know where I am! I think I've been shot down by a fish! I'm bailing out. I'm bailing out. I'm...*"

There was an almighty **splash!!!** and then a horrible

glug

glug

glug.

After that, nothing. What Tipperary did next may have been brave, but you couldn't call it sensible.

She sent us all into town to buy oilskins – those are the shiny, waterproof suits that sailors wear. She said we had to have them or we'd catch pneumonia. She said that she had one or two last minute engine bits to buy for **SOFTIE** and she'd meet us at the chippy when we'd all finished shopping.

"Forget shopping, Tipperary," I said. "Charley's in danger! We must start searching for him – now!"

"The rescue services will be doing all they can for Charley," Tipperary said. "We would only get in the way."

That didn't sound like Tipperary to me, but it's no good arguing with her, so off she went, to buy her engine bits, or so we thought, while Aunt Doris found her purse and put Hector on the lead. Hector doesn't like that so Aunt Doris only does it when she has to. She wrapped me up warm and tucked me into my buggy. She shut the hens up safely in their travelling compartment – they hate shopping – and we set off for town.

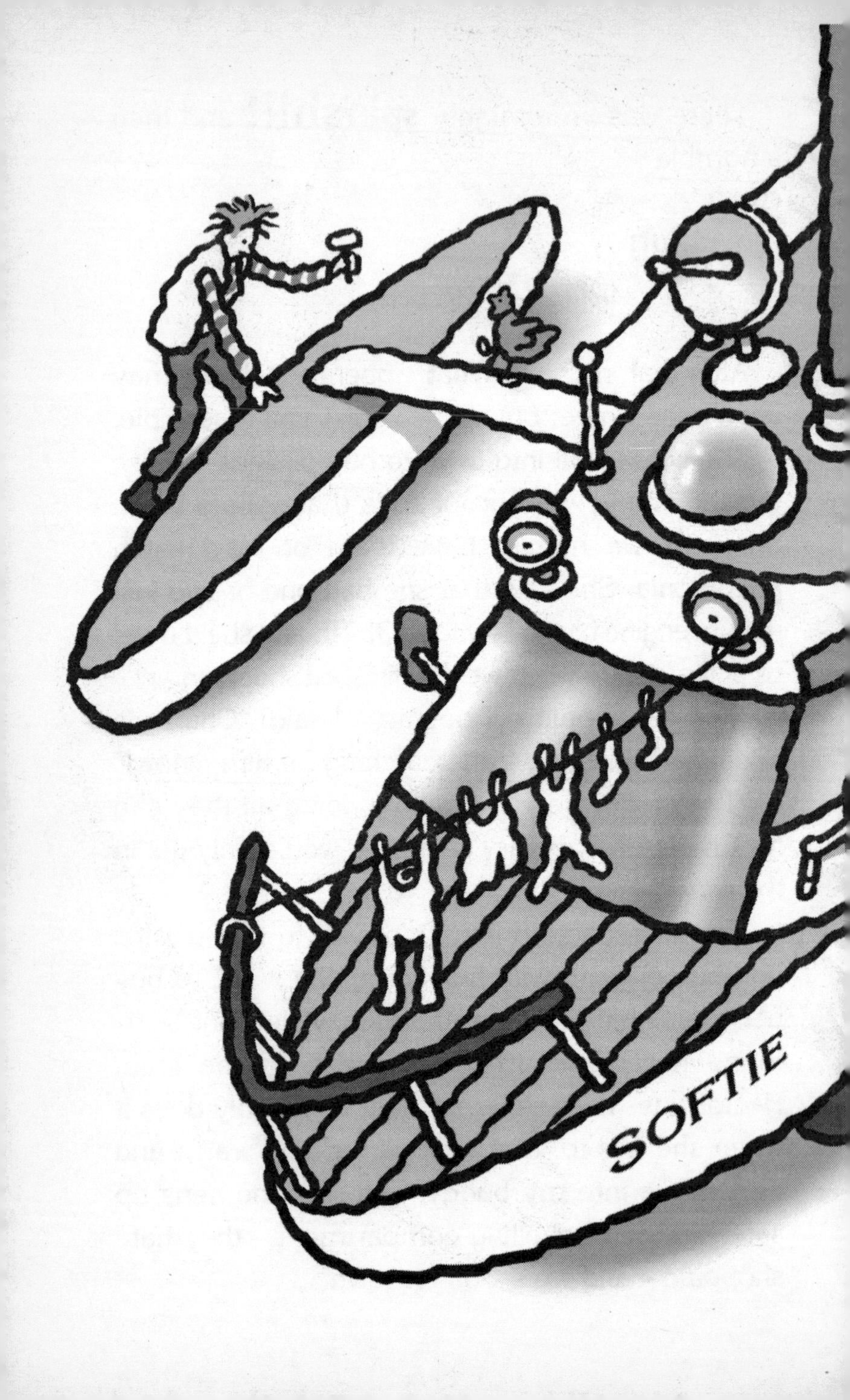
SOFTIE

We were just turning into the street where the oilskins are when all three of us had the same terrible thought. It must have been telepathy. I spat my dummy out. "*You don't think*...?" I began.

"*She wouldn't, would she*..?" Aunt Doris murmured.

"Ibetyoushejollywellhas!" Hector yelped.

He tugged his lead out of Aunt Doris's hand and bounded back the way we'd come. Aunt Doris spun my buggy round and we raced after him – by the time we got back to **SOFTIE**, my wheels were practically on fire. Aunt Doris lifted me out of the buggy and we crept aboard. Tipperary was nowhere to be seen. Hector and I hid in the cupboard under the canteen and Aunt Doris squeezed under the bunk beds, next to Bess and the hens. None of us made a sound.

We were beginning to feel pretty silly when the door opened and in jumped Tipperary. She wasn't carrying any engine bits. She sat down in the driving seat, fastened her seat belt and revved up the engine. **SOFTIE** rolled smoothly down the grassy slope and out on to the water. The retractable wheels folded up into the hull and the water wings inflated. The engine's quiet purr dropped to the baritone throb of a motor boat, and **SOFTIE**'s bows cut a foaming **'V'** through the water. We were at sea.

We stayed quiet until it was too late for Tipperary to turn round and put us ashore. Then Hector grabbed me by the collar of my babygrow – he sometimes forgets I'm not a puppy – and eased us out of the cupboard. At the same time, Aunt Doris struggled out from under the bunk bed, rubbing her knees where her arthritis was hurting. Bess and the hens stayed put under the bed, clucking in a worried sort of way. Hens don't like water and they hadn't really wanted to go to sea, but Bess had told them that it was their duty.

At first, Tipperary was concentrating so hard on her maps and charts that she didn't even notice us. Then Hector sneezed and dropped me –

I landed on his bean bag so it didn't hurt, but Tipperary nearly jumped out of her skin.

"Hector!" she shouted. "Moses!! Aunt Doris!!! You're supposed to be back at the chippy waiting for me!"

"Yes, my girl," Aunt Doris said crossly. "And it would have been a pretty long wait!"

"How could you leave us behind?" I asked. "You need us, Tipperary!"

Hector sat down and hung his head the way he does when he thinks nobody loves him. His eyes went all sad and his bottom lip wobbled. A little drool of dribble slid out of the corner of his mouth and swung below his chin.

Tipperary sighed. She bent down and kissed Hector on the top of his head. "I'm sorry," she said. "It's not that I didn't *want* you to come with me. I did. I *do*. I *know* I need you. But it's going to be so dangerous, it just didn't seem right to take you with me. If Charley's in danger – and he is – it stands to reason that I have to go. But it seemed downright wicked to risk your lives as well."

Tipperary hung her head. A tear ran down her cheek and dripped off her chin. I felt my eyes begin to sting – it always makes me cry when other people do. Hector gave me a warm wet lick and Aunt Doris put her arms round Tipperary.

"There, there," she said. "We're in this together.

And your Charley is a bright lad. He'll pull through."

There was a loud crackle and the radio went dead. The sudden silence made us all afraid. Tipperary had a good cry and so did I. When we'd finished she blew both our noses, and Aunt Doris poured two tots of whisky, one for herself and one for Tipperary. Hector and I had hot milk and biscuits. Bess and the hens crept out from under the bunk bed and pecked up the crumbs from their crumb dish.

"Are we at sea, Moses?" Bess asked. I told her that we were. "Fancy that," she said, turning to the other hens. "We're out on the ocean wave! Now, ladies: we may not be nautical by nature, but we are here to do a job and we must do our *very best*."

The hens flew up on to the canteen counter and peered nervously out of the window. I should call it a port hole, I suppose, but it still looked like an ordinary window, all smeared with salt sea spray. "How can we help, Bess?" the hens asked bravely. "You tell us what you want, and we'll do it."

"Keep a sharp lookout for Charley," Bess told them. "And for giant seafaring worms, as well," she added. "And yellow-eyed monsters." The hens looked understandably nervous but they took up their positions at each window immediately and stared out to sea in a steadfast sort of way.

Some people think hens are just egg-laying machines. They're not. Hens can fly, which is more than people can do. They can be pretty fierce when they're roused. Also they are ace at finding anything that's hidden, because of their powerful sense of smell.

At home, we don't eat eggs and we certainly don't eat hens, so we feel differently about hens and they feel differently about us. They live off in the woods by themselves, mostly, and build nests, and hatch their chicks, and look for food, and squawk a bit, and do the things birds do.

Tipperary got her maps and charts out and began to navigate. Hector sat next to her and watched, which was more helpful that it sounds, because Tipperary was feeling frightened and upset and when you feel like that, it helps to have a friend beside you. Hector looked at her with his trusty brown eyes. Every now and then he gave her a friendly shove with his wet nose, just to cheer her up. Strangely enough, it did.

By and by the radio came back on. A lady from the Coastguards was talking. "There appears to be a build-up of electricity under the sea," she said. "There have been several sightings of a large spotted sea snake, as well as what may be a hostile submarine in the Channel. All vessels return to port immediately."

Tipperary switched off the radio and turned to face us. "Now you can see why I tried to leave you behind," she said. "But since you decided to stick with me – and I'm glad you did – I think we should vote on what we do next. Do we continue the search? Or do we make for home? Aunt Doris, will you sit Moses in his bouncy chair so he can see everyone? He can translate for us."

Aunt Doris lifted me into my little bouncy chair – it's a kind of a seat on springs that Tipperary made for me. I bounced about a bit, just to relieve the tension I was feeling, while I waited to see who would speak first.

Bess fluttered up on to the table top and cleared her throat. "Ladies," she said. She looked at me and Hector. "And gentlemen," she added. I thought it was silly to call me and Hector *gentlemen*. After all, he's a dog and I'm a baby. But Bess likes to do things her way and I didn't interrupt: it's best not to, with hens. "Ladies and gentlemen. We are in peril on the sea. The sea is not a natural habitat for any of us, specially hens. But like it or lump it, we will make the best of it aboard the good ship **SOFTIE**. We have each other. Charley Cool, on the other hand, is alone in hostile waters. So I say we'd better get on and find him before this giant eel mistakes him for dinner."

Bess isn't very tactful and Tipperary looked as

though she was going to cry again, but she just sniffed and wiped her nose on her sleeve. Aunt Doris gave Tipperary a hug and said: "There, there, dear, worse things happen at sea."

"We *are* at sea, Aunt Doris," I reminded her.

"So we are, dear," Aunt Doris answered. "Well, it's just a saying. Shall we take a vote?"

"What on?" Hector asked. He hadn't been listening.

"On whether we carry on looking for Charley or go back to Portland Bill," Tipperary explained. "We must all think carefully for a moment. It's important that we all understand exactly what we're voting for." She looked hard at the hens when she said this. There was a short silence, if you don't count the thunder that was now rumbling more or less continuously, and the shriek of the wind and the roar of the waves.

"Any questions?" I asked, after I'd translated everything. There weren't.

"All in favour of staying out at sea say 'AYE'," Tipperary said.

Me and Aunt Doris said "AYE". Hector said **Rrruffff!** and the hens said "**Squarrrk!**" The vote was unanimous. We would stay at sea and try to rescue Charley.

5 "*Come to Daddy*"

"Tipperary," I said. "I want you to dangle me over the side of the boat."

"No way," said Tipperary.

"You *must*," I said.

"I *won't*."

"Certainly not, dear," said Aunt Doris. "I never heard anything so silly in all my born days."

"Stupidupidupid!" barked Hector

"Pok! Pok! Pok! Pokaaarrrkkk!" squawked Bess. Which means "Don't even *think* about it!"

"Listen," I said. "I've *got* to talk to the eel."

"I'm not dangling you over the side for any giant eel to swallow. And that's flat," Tipperary said.

"But ..." I began.

"Tipperary said NO," Aunt Doris interrupted.

"So 'No' it is. That's it and all about it, my lad."

"OK," I sighed. I know when I'm beaten. Actually, I was pretty relieved. "If you won't dangle me over, dangle something that will pick up noises from underwater and amplify my voice, so I can talk to whatever's down there."

"Fine," Tipperary said. "Give me ten minutes."

She took her CD player apart, put it together in a new way, sealed the whole thing into a polythene bag and hung it over the side. The hens watched but not even Bess offered advice. They were beginning to feel seasick. I put the headphones on and listened. At first all I could hear was the chug-chug-chug of **SOFTIE**'s engine. I asked Tipperary to turn it off and she did. It was very eerie after that. I have exceptional hearing, and I could hear all kinds of soft, musical fish voices – sort of like this: WITTE RT WITTERTW ITT E RTW ITTTTWIT ERT WITTERTWI ELVIS It was like lying in a tent when the birds are waking up outside. Deepest down and furthest away, someone big was booming. **BOVWROALA UBI BXHSZ** There were no words, just deep blue music. Closer and higher, shoals of small fish blipped and bleeped. LP BLEEPBL P BLP BLEEP BLEEPBLEEP BLPBLPBLEEP BLPPER EEEE AHAHAHA BLP P LP P It sounded like a deep sea jazz ensemble.

Then I noticed the slow, quiet throb of an engine from down below. I listened harder, and pretty soon

I heard a voice humming a mean little tune. It was a solitary, selfish sound: "*Come to Daddy, spotty face. Daddy wants you. Come to your old Daddy.*"

There was just the quiet singing of the fish for a while, and the slap slap of the waves along **SOFTIE**'s sides. Suddenly, a new voice spoke from somewhere quite close by: Darling! Come to Elvis! Where are you? Where are you hiding, dearest? I know your'e here! Speak to me beloved! Let me twine myself around your silky coils, oh, let me press you close. Speak to me! Sing to me! Give me a clue! Please, don't be shy...!

Crumbs... I thought. Because I knew at once who was talking. I had been right all along. It was a giant electric eel from outer space. His name was Elvis and he was in love with a virtual eel from CYBERFLOAT. Now what?

I cleared my throat. "Excuse me," I said. What is your name? Which means: "Excuse me. Can we talk?"

abcdefghijk he said. Which is not polite, even for an eel. I asked Aunt Doris to hold the headphones away from my ears a bit. "Could you talk a bit more quietly please, Elvis?" I asked.

"***No! I couldn't who are you anyway I don't want to talk to you I want to talk to her!!!***" he bellowed. You may have noticed that people get pretty boring when they're in love: it doesn't matter whether they're telling you about their latest boyfriend or girlfriend, or their new baby, or their pet hamster, or the football team they support, or a virtual eel from CYBERFLOAT – they get boring. Love is a wonderful thing but it doesn't necessarily make for interesting conversation.

"*Where is she*?" whined Elvis. "*I want her! I heard her sweet voice calling me. I've travelled so far to be with her. She is my destiny and I am hers. Don't torment me. If you know where she is, lead me to her.*"

"She's not here, Elvis," I said. "She's gone to Epsilon Indi."

That was unkind of me, I know. Epsilon Indi is approximately 11.4 light-years from Earth. And in case you've forgotten, an Earth light-year equals approximately 9,500,000,000,000 kilometres. So Epsilon Indi is not just round the corner by any means – though it's not so far off either, for a star.

"What did she want to go to Epsilon Indi for?" wailed Elvis. "Did she leave me a message? Did she say where she'll meet me?" Once you've started telling lies it's quite hard to stop. One lie leads to another, you get all tangled up and everything gets more and more complicated. You have to invent wilder and wilder stories.

"Yes," I lied. "She did. She said to tell you that she's crazy about you! She thinks you're fabulous. She thinks you're the eeliest eel in the ocean. She can't wait to settle down and make thousands of dear little baby eels with you. She's just a bit shy, that's all. That's why she's gone to Epsilon Indi."

Right after I said that, I wished I hadn't. One of the things that makes an eel give off electricity is hunger. When it sees dinner passing by, **ZAP!** it goes, and stuns it. Another is when it wants to say hello. **ZAP!** Another is when it's scared. **ZAP!** If it sees something coming towards it that looks fierce and scary, like your teacher (only joking) it will **ZAP** them in self-defence before they can **ZAP** it. But the thing that makes an electric eel **ZAP** the loudest and the hardest is... you guessed it... true love.

Once an electric eel starts thinking about love and romance, he's apt to blow a fuse. The buzz that eel gave when I said his lady eel was crazy about him must have blown all the other fish inside a radius of ten kilometres right out of the water. All kinds of electrical equipment was absolutely wrecked by the sudden charge – including the kind of two-way microphone that Tipperary had rigged up for me with her CD player. There was a loud hiss followed by a crackle and in the silence that followed, I heard the throb of engines coming from behind us. "Quick," I said to Tipperary. "I've *got* to keep talking to Elvis or he'll go crazy and we'll all be fried. So come on, dangle me over the side!"

Tipperary thought for a minute. Then she ran to my cot and pulled off my rubber sheet. She looked at Aunt Doris. Aunt Doris nodded and dived for her sewing box. In next to no time I had a little wet suit.

"What about your poor face?" Aunt Doris asked, blowing her nose.

"I'll try to keep it out of the water," I said.

I won't pretend I wasn't scared. Nobody *wants* to be lowered into the water with a giant electric eel. What's more, all around us the sky was turning purple with fat thunder clouds. Forked lightning whizzed and crackled and stabbed into the sea. You could hear the hiss of it and see the steam rise where it hit the water. The wind was going crazy, veering from north to south and east to west with each new roll of thunder. **SOFTIE** was lurching up and down and side to side in a horrible way. Bess and the hens lay in a huddle on Hector's beanbag, eyes shut, beaks open, moaning softly. Hector wasn't feeling too good, either. Every now and then he made a dash for the nearest window.

Aunt Doris helped me into my wet suit. She did up my life jacket and tied me to a length of good strong washing line. "Are you ready, my brave lad?" she asked in a quavering voice. I nodded. I didn't trust myself to speak. Aunt Doris wiped my nose, kissed me on the cheek, and lowered away.

It was chilly in the water, even with my wet suit on, and the waves looked like green glass hills. Each time one of them lifted me up high I could see another hundred heading straight for me. It was a cold and lonely business, bobbing up and down in the water. But what happened next was worse.

Something the colour of leopard skin began to

coil up through the water underneath me. A velvety head appeared right in front of my face. It had a beaky nose, two love-sick eyes, and an enormous droopy mouth. The eyes examined me. The mouth opened wide. A thousand pointed teeth bristled in all directions. That fish's teeth were unbelievable. He could have eaten hard boiled eggs through a tennis racquet. When he smiled, I could see inner columns of teeth marching away down his throat in the direction of his stomach. He blushed a little and his soot-and-golden skin began to glow prawn pink. When an electric eel begins to glow, look out for some shocking behaviour.

"Excuse me," I said, spluttering a bit because I'd swallowed half a wave. "*Please* don't get excited. Because if you do, you're going to give me an electric shock. And if you do that, I'll be dead. And if I'm dead, I'll never be able to tell you where *she* is."

I said it in eel, of course, which sounds like half a dozen toasters popping their fuses. Then I waited, swinging up and down in the water as the wild waves came and went, while the most tremendous struggle went on inside the heart and mind of that eel. Put yourself in his place and you'll understand. He had heard what he thought was an all-time, chart-topping love song – a mating call, if you want to be scientific – and he was simply bursting with love. All his genes were saying: *find her, court her, win her.*

Your genes, by the way, may be tiny – in fact they are – but they have a big say in how you behave. That doesn't mean that you can blame them if you burp – or worse – at table. It means that there are powerful voices somewhere inside you saying "*fall in love when you hear this sound.*" Or "*swim south when the water gets cold.*" Or "*build your nest here, in this particular tree, right now.*"

Now, that fish could hear his genes talking loud and clear. Flickers of light ran up and down the length of him. Sparks shot out and fizzed up to the surface. His little dark eyes began to glitter and a stab of lightning slipped out of his mouth like a forked tongue. "*Please,*" I said. "*Calm yourself Elvis.* Think of something else."

"I can't!" he crackled.

"*Try*!" I begged. "Say your nine times table."

"I don't know my nine times table."

"Well, say the eel alphabet backwards."

His little eyes crossed and his whole body vibrated. Gradually the flickering faded and the fizzing subsided. I breathed a deep sigh of relief, spat out half a litre of salt water and gave the thumbs-up sign to Aunt Doris, who was still

leaning out of **SOFTIE**'s window holding her breath. "Do you think Elvis would like a cup of tea, dear?" she called down. "Or a slice of cake? I could pass you some down on a tray."

"No thanks, Aunt Doris," I called up. "We're doing fine. Any news of Charley?" Aunt Doris shook her head. I turned back to Elvis.

"Listen, Elvis," I said. "Provided that you can stay calm, you and I are going to find a way to send you to Epsilon Indi."

"Can't go to Epsilon Indi. Used up almost all my energy to get here," Elvis said sadly. Tears began to trickle from his eyes and drip off his chin.

"Don't worry about that," I said. "I've already got a pretty good idea of how to do it. All we need is enough time to build you a pod."

From somewhere in the region of my stomach, which is where those feelings generally seem to start, a guilty kind of sadness was creeping up towards my chest. Was I really going to blast this love–sick eel into space? Was I really going to let him believe that he was on his way to meet the love of his life when I knew perfectly well that she was nothing more than a set of numbers in the memory of a computer? How would he feel when he got to Epsilon Indi – if he got to Epsilon Indi – and found nobody waiting for him there?

Elvis shuddered with anticipation but he didn't

send out any shocks. I put my doubts and my guilty conscience behind me for the time being. So far, so good, I thought. But deep in my heart, I knew that I was wrong.

I'll never know what made me glance up at Aunt Doris at precisely that moment, but the look I saw on her face put guilty feelings right out of my mind. Elvis was humming softly to himself with his eyes shut. He had noticed absolutely nothing. You don't, when you're in love. But the look on Aunt Doris's face said: ARRRRGGGHHHH!!!!

I looked over my shoulder. There was a yellow–eyed, skull–shaped sea monster, still under water but coming up fast right behind me! I stared into its eyes, trying to work out if it looked hungry or not. I thought that it might eat me anyway, just to see what I tasted like. Then something moved behind the yellow eyes. Something or someone. Someone horribly familiar. The yellow eyes closed. Was I looking at a sea monster, or was I looking at something worse? I was definitely looking at something worse.

6 Sleep Tight, Fishy

I realised that what I had mistaken for a sea monster was in fact a small submarine with yellow headlights and a bubble dome on top. The headlights went out when the craft reached the surface and I could see the captain inside the dome. He was no stranger to me but I had not expected to see him ever again. The last time I saw him he was driving a tank off a cliff and I was pretty confident that he'd be strawberry jam when he landed. But here he was, staring right at me through the dome of a submarine. His spidery hands crept across the control panel in front of him. He pressed a button and a mean–looking harpoon gun slid out of the front of the submarine. Silas Stoatwarden smiled and pulled the trigger.

A dart the size of a Guy Fawkes rocket buried itself in Elvis's neck. His little eyes flicked open and he stared for a second at Silas Stoatwarden. Then his eyes closed and he slid slowly down through the green water, folding down and around on himself rather like an old pair of tights, until he lay coiled in an untidy heap on the bottom of the seabed. Silas had given Elvis a massive dose of sedatives. The dart still hung from his velvety skin but Silas hadn't finished yet. A little trap door opened in the bottom of the submarine and a net the size of a football pitch drifted slowly down entangling those giant coils.

"Sleep tight, fishy," Silas crooned. "Daddy will tow you all the way to – well, never mind where to, eh? Let that be our little secret. There may be nosey-parker babies listening in."

A double-barrelled bazooka was now emerging from the submarine and it didn't look friendly. Aunt Doris hauled me up out of the water, whipped me in through the window, and dropped me, dripping, on to Hector's beanbag. Meanwhile, Tipperary used all her skill to take evasive action. Silas was no match for her. By the time he had fired his first round, we were out of range.

There was nothing we could do to free Elvis immediately. Our top priority had to be to find Charley Cool. The radio was back on now and someone from the Coastguards was shouting angrily at Tipperary because we hadn't returned to port. When the shouting died down, Tipperary asked if there was any news of Charley Cool. There was! Apparently the crew of a fishing trawler had heard singing somewhere off Tuskar Rock in the Irish Sea. They had recognised the voice at once – Charley's voice is famous, he sometimes sings the news. "Are you a fan of Charley Cool?" the Coastguard asked.

"You could say that," Tipperary replied, with a blush.

"Me too. It's too bad there was so much fog in the Irish Sea. They searched and searched but they couldn't find him."

"What was he singing?" Tipperary asked.

"*It's a Long Way to Tipperary* – a real golden oldie – I don't expect you know it."

"I know it," Tipperary answered, wiping tears of joy on her shirt sleeve. "I know it well. And so does Charley Cool."

"It makes sense, I suppose," the Coastguard said. "I mean, he would be a long way from Tipperary, wouldn't he, if he was in the Irish Sea? Tipperary's a long way inland."

"Don't be too sure about that," Tipperary answered.

"Now, I want you to turn your vessel round and head for Portland Bill. Is that understood?"

"Understood," said Tipperary.

She turned **SOFTIE** around but we did not head for Portland Bill. The wind was blowing steadily from the south and we hoisted Aunt Doris's big red sail and headed north. That afternoon found us swinging round Land's End into St George's Channel. By evening we were just off Tuskar Rock. It was there that we spotted Charley Cool. Tipperary saw him first, and burst into tears of joy. He was zipped into his survival suit and clinging to the wreckage of his helicopter. He was still singing at the top of his voice.

A giant grin lit up his face when he saw **SOFTIE** chugging towards him through the choppy sea. Every now and then a monster wave would hide us from each other and once Charley was almost swept away by the huge waves bursting all around him and the cold wind scouring his frozen face and hands. We came as close alongside him as we dared and threw out a life belt on a rope. Charley pulled it on and clipped himself into the safety harness while Tipperary dropped a rope ladder out of **SOFTIE**'s back window.

That's when I knew I wasn't going to send poor old Elvis, if he ever got away from Silas Stoatwarden, off on a wild goose chase to Epsilon Indi. When I saw the look of joy on Tipperary's face, and the way Charley's love beamed right back to her, I understood that love is not something to be sent off half-way across the galaxy just because it suits us to send it there. Charley climbed aboard and fell dripping into Tipperary's arms. Aunt Doris wrapped a warm blanket around the two of them and we all tactfully watched seagulls through the window while Tipperary cried buckets in Charley's arms.

With Charley safe and well and back on board, Tipperary reported his rescue to the Coastguard. The Coastguard was not pleased. She had been looking forward to finding Charley herself, and maybe getting his autograph. "Since you have Mr Cool aboard," she said, "I'll escort you back to harbour. Wait for me exactly where you are."

We didn't, of course. With Charley safe, we were free to search for Elvis. He shouldn't be hard to find – once the sedatives wore off, he would be sending out shocks like – well, like a huge electric eel. What we had not taken into account was just how long Silas Stoatwarden could keep him asleep. Without Bess the Buff Orpington and her special powers I don't think we would ever have found him.

Did I mention to you that hens are good at finding things, because of their keen sense of smell? Not just anything, mind you. Hens are not interested in roses or sweet peas. Hens are interested in food. And to a hungry hen, a giant eel smells like a lot of food. I don't think Bess knew the extent of her own powers, and if she hadn't fallen overboard we might never have discovered them either.

It happened like this: Bess was still feeling dreadfully queasy; she was longing for everything to stop going up and down and just keep still for a while. She begged us to put her ashore on Tuskar Rock and let her feel dry land between her claws, if only for a few minutes. The other hens wanted what Bess wanted – they usually did – but Tipperary said she couldn't do it, it was just too dangerous. The wind roars round those rocks night and day and a hen could be swept into the sea in the twinkling of an eye. Besides which, **SOFTIE** could be rammed by a wave and break up on the rocks. By way of a compromise, Tipperary agreed to let the hens spend an hour or two on deck, provided they allowed Aunt Doris to tie them to the railings with good strong string. Well, they'd only been up there for about ten minutes when we hit an extra big wave, there was a bloodcurdling squaaarrrkkkkox. An egg shot past the window followed by half a dozen hens.

There are few sights more miserable than six wet hens. We hauled them out of the sea and sat them by the heater. Aunt Doris fluffed up their feathers on a soft towel while Charley dripped drops of medicinal whisky down their beaks. When they could speak again, Bess fluttered nimbly up on to the table and addressed us.

"Listen," she said. "While I was down there in the water," – here she paused and a shiver shook her feathers – "I discovered something important. You all know that I can smell a worm that thinks it's safe and sound fifteen centimetres underground. You know that I can dig up a crust of bread that's been hiding in the compost heap for a fortnight. And you know that no juicy caterpillar is safe from my beak, not if it's hiding half a kilometre away."

That bit about the caterpillar was an exaggeration, but I let it pass. "Well," Bess went on, fanning her feathers excitedly, "when I was in the water I'm absolutely certain that I could smell that overgrown lummox of an eel. I'm sure I caught a whiff of Silas, too."

"Bess!" I exclaimed. "That's great! Can you tell us which way he went?"

"Easy," said Bess, pointing due north with her beak. "They went that way."

Tipperary set the controls for due north and Charley cooked us a special seafood soup. We all had some, even Hector. He's a pretty messy eater and by the time he'd finished lapping his soup out of his bowl he had soup all over his face, soup behind his ears, soup under his chin and soup on all four paws. I don't know how he does it. Aunt Doris fed me mine in sips from a teaspoon and apart from one small dribble and a sneeze I made no mess at all.

After supper, what with being absolutely full of seafood soup, I fell asleep in Hector's Comfy Dog–Eze basket. I didn't wake up until he got in, too, and sat down on my head. It was dark by then, even when he moved off my head. Aunt Doris and the hens were dozing on the bunk beds. Charley and Tipperary were standing by the window staring out to sea, their arms around each other.

Underneath us and all round us, **SOFTIE**'s powerful engine chugged steadily as we rocked our way north towards the Mull of Kintyre.

Charley was talking quietly to Tipperary. "Tipp," he said, gently.

"Yep?" answered Tipperary.

"About that stuff I told you before. When you were asleep."

"What about it, Charley?"

"Well. It's not easy to say. But I've got to try or I'll burst."

"Better speak up then," said Tipperary.

"I've never met anyone like you, Tipperary. There isn't anyone like you. I'm mad about you, Tipp. I want to spend my life with you. I want to circumnavigate the globe by hang–glider with you for co–pilot. I want to cross the Sahara desert on a camel with you. I want to walk the Silk Road from Transylvania to the Gobi Desert with you. I want to snowboard off the top of Mount Everest with you. I want to catch the waves on Big Sur with you for ever. Because I love you, Tipperary. I love you. Do you love me?"

There was a long, long silence. All you could hear was the quiet lap–lap of the waves on **SOFTIE**'s hull, the sough of the wind, and a soft, sweet snore. Tipperary was fast asleep. Charley sighed and climbed into his sleeping bag.

7 Brave Bess

First light found us with Donaghadee to the west of us and the Mull of Galloway to the east. A steady wind filled our sail and bowled us along at double the speed our engine could have managed on its own.

Whenever Bess felt she was losing track of Elvis, that brave chicken made us lower her into the water so that she could take a good strong sniff. Aunt Doris wrapped her in a large sou'wester each time – that's a waterproof hat – to keep the worst of the water off her feathers, but even so it must have been a frightening and uncomfortable experience for her. We could tell that it took every last bit of her courage.

We sailed north on the trail of Elvis for a day and a night. We knew that he was still drugged and helpless because if he hadn't been, we would have seen fireworks lighting up the sky as he blasted Silas Stoatwarden into orbit with a series of mighty electric shocks. From time to time Aunt Doris lifted me up and showed me where we were on the map. "If we don't stop soon," she said, "we'll be in Iceland. I shall have to get knitting."

"Maybe Silas wants to freeze Elvis," I said. "Keep him on ice, sort of."

"But why?" asked Charley. "What's he planning?"

"You know he's mad about anything from space," I said. "That's why he wanted me – so he could do experiments on me and find out how I work. He wouldn't find out much – I'm just the same as any other baby, when I'm here."

"I don't know about that, dear," Aunt Doris said. "You're not like any baby I've looked after. You get a lot more wind, for a start, And you're rather on the brainy side."

"Well," I said, trying to get back to the point – it isn't always easy with Aunt Doris – "Stoatface knows that Elvis is from space. And that's enough to make him want to do all sorts of nasty things to him. Besides, in the wrong hands, Elvis could be a deadly weapon. Stoatface's hands are definitely the wrong ones and you know how he feels about deadly weapons. He's just mad about them."

Off in the north–west, in the direction of Rockall, lay a scatter of islands. "What are those?" I asked. "I can't see them on the map." Tipperary fetched out a large-scale chart and scanned it carefully.

"That's odd," she said. "They don't seem to be marked on here."

"**Pok pok pok squarrrkkkk!!!**" Bess hollered. And then "Pok pok pok Squrrrokkkkxx!!!"

"Yes, dear," Aunt Doris said. "We understand. You don't care if they're marked on the map or not, do you dear?"

"**Pk! pk! pk! Paaarrrkkkk!!!**"

"Elvis is on the left–hand island," I translated.

Hector came out from underneath his beanbag and sniffed the sea breeze. Pretty soon he began to bark and bounce simultaneously. It's very difficult for a dog to do one without the other and Hector certainly couldn't manage it. "**Bigeelbigeel bigbigbigeel!!!**" he barked.

"Hector can smell him, too," I told the others.

"Good dog!" Charley nodded. "Well done, Hector!"

"**Dogbiscuitsdogbiscuitsdogbiscuits!**" Hector barked happily.

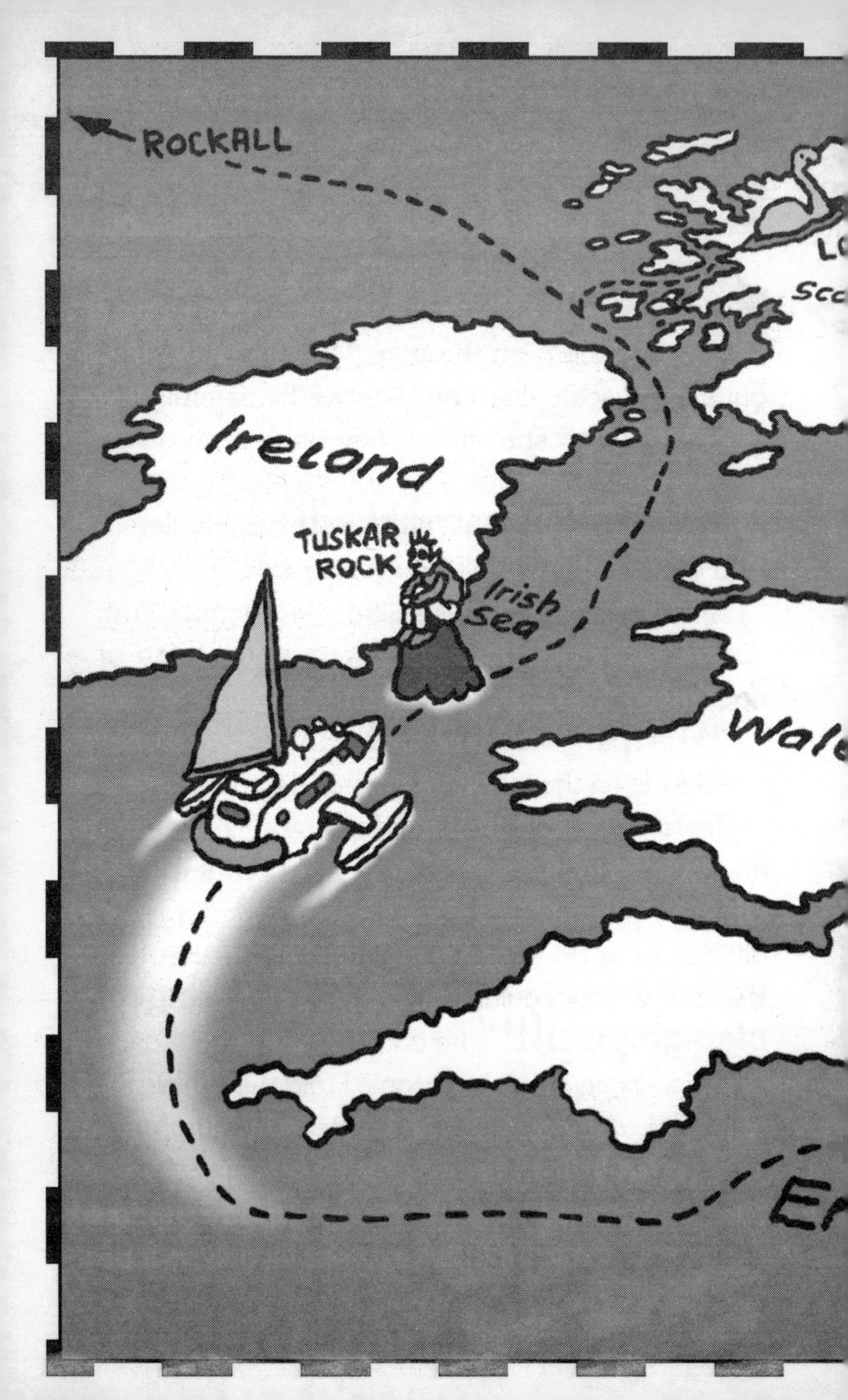

ROCKALL
Ireland
TUSKAR ROCK
Irish Sea

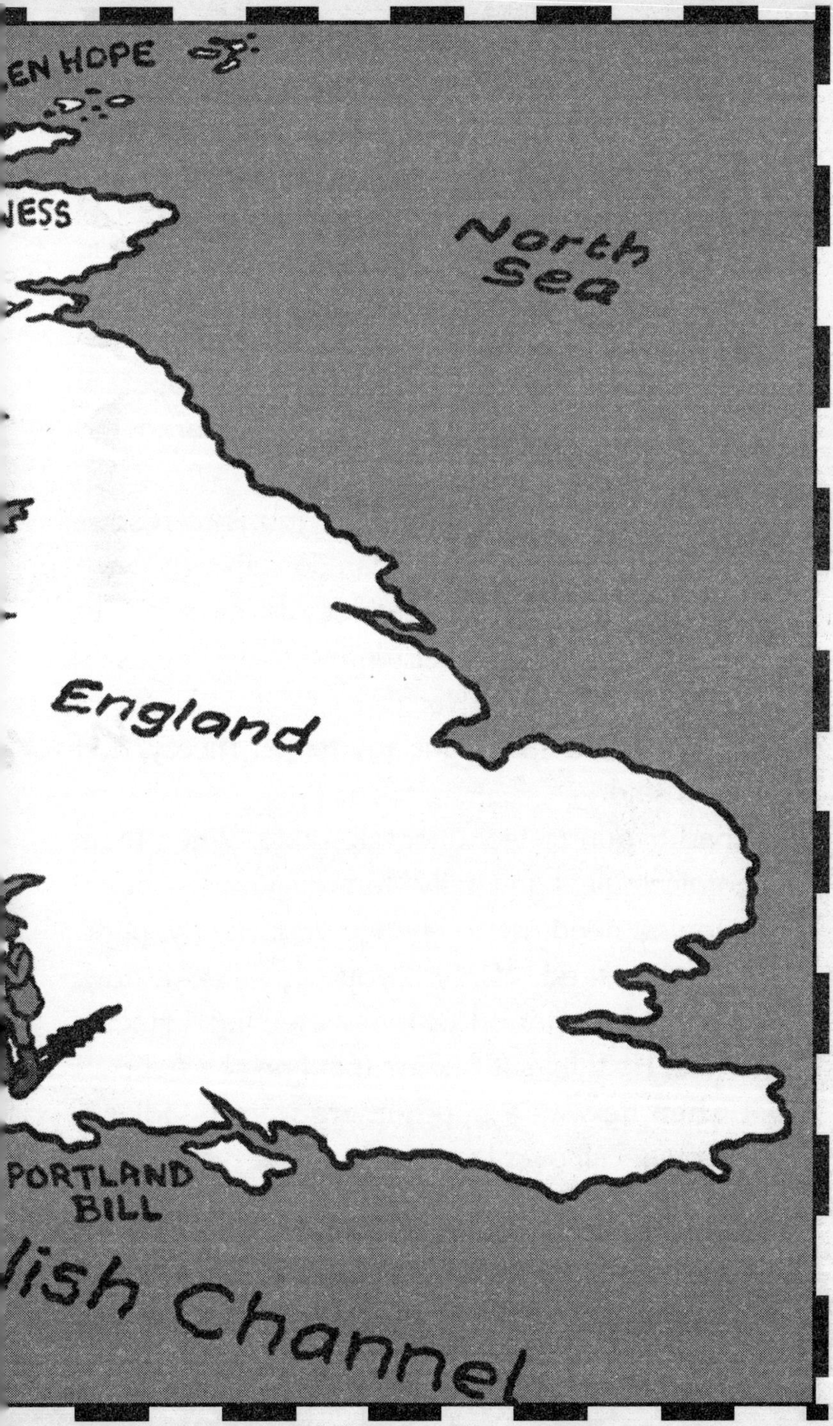

EN HOPE

NESS

North Sea

England

PORTLAND BILL

lish Channel

Bess stopped squawking and cleared her throat. "I think it's time we made a plan," she said quietly. "We'd better sit down and talk things out."

We sat down round the table. Aunt Doris poured a drop of milk for Hector, put some dandelion and burdock in my bottle, and mixed up a dish of warm bran mash for the hens. She poured three tots of whisky – one for herself, one for Tipperary and one for Charley Cool – and declared the meeting OPEN.

"As I see it," she began, "our job is to rescue Elvis. I don't know what we can do with him, once we've rescued him, but we can't just leave him to Silas Stoatwarden's tender mercy."

"Why not?" asked Hector.

"Because he hasn't got any tender mercy, dog brain," I said.

I had begun to feel uncomfortable. When I feel uncomfortable, I generally start to wriggle.

"Do you need me to change your nappy, pet?" Tipperary asked. "Only if you do, I'll do it now, and then we'll get on with our meeting." Hector smirked. He thinks it's funny that I need a nappy. I bet when he was a puppy there were puddles – and worse – all over the floor.

"No thanks," I said. "I'm perfectly clean and dry."

"Whyareyouwrigglingthen?" asked Hector, rudely.

"Because of what I told poor Elvis," I replied. "I feel so mean. I told him the eel of his dreams is up on Epsilon Indi. I've worked out how to send him there and he'll go, I know he will. He's longing to be with his true love. But how's he going to feel when he gets to Epsilon Indi? He's going to be so lonely up there. Nobody lives there now, they all left years ago. I feel so sorry for him, now that I'm not scared of him."

There was a long silence round the table. We were all imagining exactly how Elvis would feel when he found out we'd tricked him. First, we imagined his longing to find the one he loved. Then we imagined his tremendous joy and delight when he thought he was about to fold her in his loving coils. Then we imagined his miserable, sad, lonely feelings when he found out that she wasn't there. Never had been. Never would be. We sighed. Several of the hens shed a tear. Even Hector looked gloomy.

It was no good. We just couldn't do it. All of us knew, before any of us spoke. It just wouldn't be right.

"Well," said Aunt Doris. "That's that, then. We can't send him to wherever-you-said, Moses. So we'll just have to think of something else to do with him."

There was another long silence, apart from a

few gurgly noises, which you can't help with dandelion and burdock. Everyone seemed to be listening hard to something. Just at first, we didn't realise what was happening. Then, gradually, it dawned on us. Nobody was speaking but we could all communicate. We weren't hearing each other exactly – at least not word for word, not even thought for thought. We were getting the flavour of each other's ideas without using words at all. It was a very special moment.

"Holy Moley!" Tipperary breathed. "What's happening? Moses, is this anything to do with you?"

"Yes," I said, modestly. "I think it must be. It's just telepathy. It happens all the time at home. I think you must have caught it from me." The rest of that meeting went really fast. It does, when you don't have to talk. We made a terrific plan. Perhaps telepathy will work between us, now – you and me. Let's try.

Did you get all of that? I hope you did. That way, I needn't waste time explaining the plan.

8 Flying High

Everything was decided and everyone knew exactly what they had to do. Charley opened a window and leaned out. He licked his finger and held it up to see which way the wind was blowing.

"It's from south to north with a bit of west in it, little buddy," he told me. "Which is exactly what we want. Aunt Doris? How's that papoose pouch coming?"

"Aw–ows eddy," Aunt Doris answered, speaking round a mouthful of pins. She was double stitching the seams to make them double strong. Tipperary packed wet suits, flippers, sandwiches, rusks and a dry nappy into Charley's backpack. Emergency supplies were stowed in the bottom of my papoose pouch. It was time to go.

Charley buckled on his flying harness. He had painted his batwing grey, with one or two dark clouds for camouflage and it looked beautiful, just like a piece of sky. He slid me into my papoose pouch and strapped me firmly to his chest. I was facing outwards and downwards, so I would get a real bird's-eye view of our flight. "You're gonna love this, little buddy," Charley said excitedly.

Personally, I wasn't too sure. I won't pretend I wasn't scared. Flying in a pod is one thing. Flying in a papoose pouch strapped to Charley's chest is something else.

Tipperary kissed us goodbye, Hector licked us goodbye and the hens wished us luck. I think Bess could tell that I was scared. "Flying's easy," she said, encouragingly. "There's nothing to it. You'll love it, Moses." Aunt Doris patted my cheek. She didn't say anything, you could tell she felt too choked.

Charley stood on deck, rocking slightly on his toes. He took a deep breath. So did I. Then the batwing unfurled above our heads and the wind lifted us off the deck and swept us out across the wild green sea. Charley found a thermal – that's a rising current of warm air – within seconds, and it carried us up and away, wheeling like an albatross. **SOFTIE** and Tipperary and Aunt Doris and Hector and Bess and the hens dwindled to

dots and finally to nothing. The sea looked smooth and flat and solid, like a snooker table. The islands, those strange islands that weren't on Tipperary's map, looked like fly specks. When we were hanging high above them, Charley slid us off the thermal and we began to swoop down the wind, circling towards the island Bess said was THE ONE. It was like being a bird – I felt wild and free and frightened. I loved it. I wanted it to last for ever.

The island was small and round and heathery, with a mountain in the middle and a rim of rocks running out into the sea. We could see Stoatwarden's submarine at the end of a little pier. Beside it, in the shallow water, we could see a tangled mass of netting. Poor Elvis was coiled round and round inside it, hopelessly muddled up and still deep asleep. Silas Stoatwarden was leaning over the side of the pier poking him with a stick.

Charley took us in behind the mountain so that Stoatface wouldn't see us and we landed half-way up, with a bump. He folded up his wing and put it in his backpack. Then he sat down on a rock and fished the sandwiches and rusks out of the papoose pouch. His peanut butter and banana sandwiches were a bit squishy, because I had been sitting on them, but my rusks were fine. Flying makes you hungry. I ate all my rusks and a pot of stewed apple and I tried a corner of Charley's sandwich, too.

When I felt nice and full, I sat on Charley's lap and concentrated hard. I was trying to make telepathic contact with Elvis but it was absolutely hopeless. For a start, we didn't know each other well enough. Even if we had, all I would have heard from inside his brain would have been **ZzzzzZZzzzzz.**

"Never mind," Charley said. "We'll just have to wait until old Stoatface goes to sleep. It'll be dark in a few hours and he's bound to drop off then. I may as well change your nappy while we're waiting, and then we'll have a game of cards."

Charley loves cards. So do I. We use buttons for money, usually, but this time we used pebbles. Small ones were worth 10p. Middle-sized ones were worth 50p. Great big heavy ones were worth £1. By the time it was getting dark I must have owed Charley about £5000. I explained to him that I only get fifty pence a week pocket money, so it would take me ten thousand weeks to pay him back – and that was if I didn't buy anything for myself at all. Ten thousand weeks is quite a long time not to buy yourself *anything*. I think it's a hundred and ninety-two years. Charley said not to worry, he was a patient man.

Meanwhile, Stoatface was putting up his tent. He made a real botch job of it, it took him ages. Once it was more or less up he lit a little camping gas stove, opened a couple of tins and tipped them into a saucepan. When his supper was warm he spooned it straight from the pan. Then, without even doing the washing-up, he crawled inside his tent. His torch glowed softly for a while before the tent went dark.

9 Swimming South

Charley tucked me back into my papoose pouch and we set off down the mountain. Pretty soon we could hear Silas Stoatwarden snoring. So far, so good. When we got down close to the shore we could hear Elvis snoring, too. We tiptoed past the tent and out on to the pier – at least Charley tiptoed, I was nestled down inside the pouch. Charley crept stealthily along the pier. His trainers didn't make a sound. At the end, he sat down with his legs dangling over the edge and lowered me carefully into the inky dark water. It was cold half-in and half-out of the sea, but it was not as cold as it would have been if my pouch had leaked – I had asked Aunt Doris to wrap it in rubber, because I was pretty sure that at some point I was going to have to get into the water. It's lucky that Aunt Doris is so good at sewing.

Elvis's big, sleepy, leopard-skin face looked peaceful. Now and then his eyes twitched slightly as he dreamed of love and romance. He shifted his coils slowly, trying in his sleep to find a comfortable way to lie, tangled up as he was in the net. I couldn't help feeling sorry for him, and a bit guilty, too, when his huge mouth curled into a happy smile. I guessed he was dreaming of his journey to Epsilon Indi, and of the meeting that would make his dreams come true.

"Excuse me," I whispered – in eel of course. "I'm sorry to disturb you Elvis. But could you wake up?" Nothing happened. "*Epsilon Indi,*" I whispered. He stirred and opened one eye.

"G'way," he murmured. "I wan'sleep."

"No you don't," I whispered. "You want to wake up. You've been shot full of sleeping pills and you're a prisoner. If you want to get away, you'd better wake up."

Elvis snored.

"I don't want to rush you, little buddy," Charley said from up above my head. "But Stoat-features has just switched his torch on."

"*Epsilon Indi,*" I whispered. "*Dream lover.*"

Elvis's coils rippled gently. A flicker of blue light ran up and down his spine. "Steady," I whispered.

"Listen. I haven't got much time. My friend Charley is going to cut you loose, so don't **ZAP** him. OK? Just listen carefully and do exactly what I say."

Charley slid into the water beside me and began to cut through a section of the net. "What's Silas up to?" I whispered.

"Judging by his shadow on the tent," Charley whispered back, "he's searching for his socks. Now he's found them. Now he's looking for his boots. Got one. Can't find the other. No – got it. I'd say we've got about a minute while he does them up, Moses."

"Get cutting, Charley," I whispered. Then I turned to Elvis. "As soon as Charley's cut a big enough hole in the net," I said, "you must swim south. Head back towards Ireland. Wait for us off the Giant's Causeway. You'll recognise it by the weird rocks if you put your head out of the water and look. But don't let anyone see you. We'll meet you there and take you to a safe place."

"What about the giant?" Elvis asked nervously.

"He won't be there," I said. "Just do it. Go!"

Half a kilometre of leopard-skin-coloured electric eel shot out to sea in a straight line, fizzing and sparking with excitement as he tasted freedom – just as Silas Stoatwarden came stamping along the pier above our heads. His torch flickered down on to the water.

"You again!" he snarled. "What have you done with my eel? That eel was my private property!"

Charley slid into the water beside me. Silas drew a pistol from his pocket and pointed it at me and Charley.

"You with the hair," he said to Charley. "Get out of the water. And bring the little nosey–parker with you."

"Shut your eyes, little buddy," Charley whispered into my ear. "And hold your nose. We're gonna dive."

The night was dark, which was lucky because it meant that Silas couldn't see where to shoot. But I didn't think we'd last long, even so. The water was so cold and I didn't see how Charley could tell which direction to swim in. Maybe he couldn't, but when we came up from our dive he took off fast, doing a powerful backstroke so as to keep my face out of the water. We soon left Stoatwarden behind, though we could hear him shouting.

We were both close to freezing and Charley was pretty well exhausted when the water fizzed and bubbled round us and something enormously strong, something like a giant squidgy tree trunk, rose up underneath us and simply lifted us out of the water.

"Where to?" asked Elvis.

"Can you find **SOFTIE**?" I asked him.

"Easy," he told me. "I can follow the vibrations of her motor."

That was the most extraordinary ride. Elvis swam almost on the surface of the water, his long body sweeping steadily from side to side. Charley rode him like a bucking bronco, gripping the slithery black and golden skin with his knees and keeping both his arms wrapped tightly around me. Silas was soon left far behind.

The eel's long body cut through the water with a swish swish sound, throwing up sparkling curtains of water that glittered when the moon came out. Sometimes he seemed to leap clear of the sea and skim the surface like a fish. It was terrifying and exciting all at the same time, better even than flying, and I wanted it never to stop.

A big old basking shark swam alongside us for a little way, then *harrumphed* like an elephant and dived. We found ourselves passing through a flotilla of jelly creatures like umbrellas with trailing tentacles – Charley said they were Portuguese men-of-war. They seemed to be arguing about something, but Portuguese is one of the very few languages I don't speak, so I couldn't tell what it was about. Charley drew his legs up like a jockey so they wouldn't sting him and we left them behind.

10 Captured

Not long after that, Elvis felt the vibrations of Silas's submarine behind us. He put on a tremendous spurt of speed, but no creature can swim at top speed for long. One minute we were slicing through the water singing *My Bonnie Lies Over the Ocean* and the next, Silas Stoatwarden was rising from the sea right behind us, water pouring off the dome of his submarine as he surfaced, his harpoon gun already trained on Elvis. The second the dart hit Elvis's neck, we felt him relax underneath us, and he began to sink, leaving us floating on the surface. But not for long: two things happened at once – a net shot out of the back of the submarine and wrapped itself round Elvis and a pair of pincers like giant lobster claws poked out at the front and grabbed me. The dome opened and I was drawn inside the submarine, while Charley, was left bobbing up and down in his life jacket. The last I saw of him was a brown hand waving.

"Got you both," smiled Silas with an ugly leer. He bent to pat a mean–looking dog that was dribbling on his shoes. It's not often you see a nasty-looking dog, is it? Sometimes you see one who has been badly treated and he will look sad or angry, but mostly they're cheerful souls. This dog was not a cheerful soul. He was not the friendly sort, and he was not the sort who's been badly treated. He was the just–plain–nasty sort. He was big, a good bit bigger than an Alsatian. His fur was dirty and there wasn't much of it. His tail was long and straggly and he had more than his fair share of teeth and claws. But the strangest thing about him was his eyes. They were red. Definitely red. When he saw me he padded over and stuck his nose right in my face. His breath smelled worse than old socks.

Silas smiled his nastiest smile. "Well my little friend," he said, "now for a long and interesting talk." The dog smirked and gargled in a menacing kind of way. "Leave him, Vulper!" Silas snapped. "He's not your dinner. Yet." I felt glad about that. I would hate to be Vulper's dinner.

I was terribly worried about Charley, up on the surface of the wild, cold sea, but there wasn't time to worry for long. "Let's get down to business, baldie," Silas said, propping me up and pouring himself a drink. He didn't offer me one.

"I haven't got any business with you, Silas Stoatwarden," I replied. "And if you don't want a whole lot of trouble you'd better let me and Elvis go. The Coastguards are looking for me and so are my friends and if they find you've taken me prisoner, there'll be trouble."

"They won't," Silas replied. "And anyway, you started it. You stole my eel."

"He's not *your* eel."

"I suppose he's your eel, is he?"

"Of course not. He doesn't belong to anyone. He's just here on a visit."

"Like my friend Vulper," Silas agreed.

I looked across at Vulper. Somehow he didn't seem like an ordinary dog. *Here on a visit,* Silas had said. So that was it. Vulper wasn't an ordinary dog. Vulper was an alien, like me. He was a Vulpeculan, from the Constellation of the Fox. You can find Vulpecula on any star chart, not far from Altair, but not many travellers choose to go there. It's got a bad reputation.

"Yes," said Silas, although I hadn't spoken. "That's right. He's from out there, too. Like you and the eel. And all three of you are going to help me with a little plan I have. You're not the only one who likes space travel, baldie. It must be obvious to any one but a fool, that the first man to get a good-sized gun set up in space will have enormous power. Well, I intend to get out there and make history. Once my plan has worked, I shall be able to take whatever I want, and plenty of it. Nobody will be able to stop me. I am going to be the most powerful person in the world and you are going to help me."

"No way, José," I said, trying to sound nonchalant. "What makes you think I'd want to help you?"

"Oh, I think you will," he smiled. "I think you'll find that Vulper here can be very persuasive." Vulper showed me two rows of horrible yellow teeth and drooled.

"What's he promised you, Vulper?" I asked. "He won't keep his promises, you know. People like him never do."

"Vulper be Emperor of Vulpecula. Great big important Emperor Vulper, His Highness. Everybody do what I say. Vulper be Very Important Dog. Eat lots of bones."

"Don't be daft," I said. "Even a dump like Vulpecula wouldn't have a scruffy mutt like you for Emperor."

"Will too."

"Won't."

"Silas said."

"Silas is a liar. How did you get here, anyway?" I asked. Vulper didn't answer; he was sulking.

"I sent for him," Silas told me, proudly. "I've

been in communication with Vulpecula for some time. Vulper here was one of my more successful ideas."

"I don't know much about dogs," I said, "but I wouldn't call him a success. I'd call him a disaster." Vulper crossed his eyes, put his ears back, and gargled a bit in the back of his throat.

11 Loch Ness

I can't remember much about the journey that followed. It passed in a haze of Vulper's bad breath and Silas's gloating threats as he tried to make me tell where **SOFTIE** was. He was determined to sink her with his big bazooka. It's a good thing I didn't know, otherwise I might have given in and told him.

After what seemed like ages, we surfaced at a wild, deserted part of the coast, all rocks and heather and stunted, windswept rowan trees. Parked at the end of a bumpy track, looking as out of place as a goldfish in clover, stood a large, articulated lorry with a powerful-looking winch on the back. Silas had hired it in Fort William and arranged for it to be waiting here for him. The back was empty except for a canoe and some diving gear. Silas winched Elvis into the back of the lorry, coil by coil. Elvis didn't bat an eyelid. He was deep asleep. Once he was all curled up in the back of the lorry, Silas pushed me in on top of him and slammed the door.

We bumped off down the track, with me slipping and sliding between Elvis's mighty coils. It was pitch dark inside the lorry and I felt scared and hungry. All I'd had to eat was one of Vulper's dog biscuits and a few sips of water out of Vulper's dog bowl and the journey seemed to take for ever. Each time we went up-hill or down-hill, I heard the growl of the lorry's gears, and the hiss of its brakes. When at last it stopped and Silas got me out, we were in a lonely place with woods at our backs and a big expanse of cold dark water in front of us. "Welcome to Loch Ness," smirked Silas Stoatwarden.

Getting a confused and sleepy Elvis out of the back of the lorry and into the water, still entangled in his net, wasn't easy. Two children picking flowers by the canal side heard a slither, looked up, and saw a kilometre of leopard-skin-coloured eel all tangled up in a net the size of a football pitch. They dropped their flowers and screamed. Their mother came running to see what was wrong but by the time she got to them, Elvis had disappeared below the surface of the loch and all that could be seen was Silas, standing by his lorry with a smile on his face. The children told their mother what they'd seen and they got a good telling-off for fibbing. Why is it called a *good* telling off? There's nothing good about getting told off, is there? It's horrible. Especially when you haven't done what you're being told off *for*. Even when you have, there's nothing *good* about it.

As soon as there was nobody about, Silas hauled the canoe and the gear out of the lorry. He bundled first me and then Vulper into our diving gear. He didn't care a bit about twisting my arms to get them in the sleeves, or bending my fingers back when he was pulling my arms through. He didn't care about the fasteners scratching my face when he pulled the mask thing on over my head. He was just as rough and thoughtless getting Vulper into his suit too. Vulper had a suit, with weights on the paws and a mask, just like a person's diving suit but with four legs instead of two, and a tail. The masks had little intercoms inside so we could talk to one another underwater.

When we were all trussed up in our diving gear, Silas told Vulper to get into the canoe. Vulper didn't want to but he could tell he'd got no choice. I didn't want to get in either, but Silas dumped me in on top of Vulper. He launched the canoe on to the water, hopped in himself, and paddled us out towards the middle of the loch – that's what a lake is called in Scotland.

Presently, we came up alongside a floating orange buoy. Silas moored the canoe to the buoy and strapped me on to Vulper's back. We dived.

It was murky and gloomy underwater and I couldn't help being afraid. I was still very hungry and inside my rubber diving suit I had what felt like a truly awful nappy. It was itching dreadfully. But once we got down to the bottom, among the waving green weeds and the sleepy ground-floor fishes, something came in view that made my itches and fears vanish. A silver rocket, about the height of three houses one on top of the other, stood on the bottom of Loch Ness. It was the most beautiful piece of engineering I had ever seen.

"That's my baby," smirked Silas. "Not bad, eh?"

"You built that?" I asked. "*You* did?" I couldn't quite believe that someone as horrible as Silas could have built something as beautiful as the rocket – or that something that was meant to do nothing but harm could look so good. But Silas nodded.

"That's right," he said. "The gun's in the nose. It's powerful enough to blast whole cities in one

glorious go. I can wipe out Wales, scorch Scotland, and fry the rest of this pathetic island any time I want to. I can melt the ice caps and put half the coastlines of the world underwater. I can turn forests into deserts. I can do *what* I want, *when* I want. From now on, *everybody* can do what I want, when I want. Or fry."

"You're mad," I said. "And I'm not going to help you." I sounded quite brave, but in my heart I doubted that I could stand up to Vulper, if he was told to persuade me.

Meanwhile, Silas had allowed Elvis to sink down to the bottom of the loch, still tangled up in his net, but beginning to wake up. "Got to get this big fish loaded fast," Silas told Vulper. "Once he wakes up we'll never get him aboard."

"You're sending Elvis into space?" I asked. "Aboard your rocket?"

"He's our fuel, baldie," Silas replied. "We're going to bung him in the fuel tank. Once he gets angry enough he'll spark up, big time. Mine is going to be the first electric-eel-powered rocket in space. Neat idea, eh?" Silas began to pour Elvis into the fuel tank. It was rather like watching someone get into a tight pair of jeans. He shifted a little here and a little there. He wriggled a bit. And then he settled. His big face looked out from a round porthole and he smiled.

He had no idea what was going on.

Silas kicked back up to the surface leaving me strapped to Vulper's bony back at the bottom of the loch. I decided to ignore Vulper. It was time to tell Elvis the truth. I couldn't let him blast off into space believing what I'd told him – about his true love being up on Epsilon Indi. It would be too cruel. I knew I had to tell him that his true love didn't exist, that she was just a set of numbers in the memory of a computer, and not a real live eel with a heart full of love. But I wasn't sure how to begin.

Elvis squirmed uncomfortably in the fuel tank. He was waking up.

"Am I going to Epsilon Indi?" he asked hopefully.

"Well, no ..." I said.

"Why not?" he asked.

I sighed. "You've been asleep a long while, Elvis. You were captured by Silas Stoatwarden and drugged. He's loaded you on to his rocket and now he's waiting for you to blast off with a barrage of mega–shocks. He's mad, Elvis. He's got a huge gun in the nose of the rocket. He wants to rule the world. You must try very hard not to spark up. OK?"

Elvis nodded.

"What I have to tell you isn't going to be easy

for you to understand. It isn't going to be easy for me to explain, but I've got to try. Before I start, I want you to promise me something."

"Promise you what?" .

"Promise not to lose your temper," I said. "However cross you feel, you must try to control yourself and not start making electricity. Otherwise you'll blast off into space and Silas Stoatwarden will have won. He'll rule the world. Do you promise?" Elvis nodded.

"The thing is, Elvis," I began, "sometimes, when you want something very, very badly, and you find you can't have it, you feel angry and upset and miserable. Don't you?"

Elvis closed his eyes, shook his large head, and blinked. "Moses," he said quietly. "If you've got something to tell me, just tell me. I don't want your philosophy. I don't want your psychology. So put a sock in it. OK?"

"OK," I said. I gulped. "The sound you heard, and fell in love with, wasn't made by an eel. It was just a sound effect on a computer game. There's nobody on Epsilon Indi. I lied to you. I'm sorry."

I was expecting fireworks. I was expecting him to fizz and thrash and spark up a storm, but what really happened was far worse. Elvis looked at me through his small round porthole for a few seconds. Two silver tears welled from his eyes and rolled down his velvet cheeks. A rippling shudder travelled down his body and a deep and painful throb of misery burst from him. It burst silently, because that's how eels cry, but it shook him from his nose down to his tail. Then he turned his great head away from me. I could tell that he was saying goodbye to the first, best dream of his life.

"D'you want to talk?" I asked, after a while. He shook his head and we stayed there, together but in silence, for a long while. From somewhere far above the cold water of Loch Ness came the wild skirl of a solitary piper. "Elvis," I said, eventually. "We've got to get you out of there. Otherwise Silas will blast you into space and it will be horrible for you and he will be the ruler of the world, which will be horrible for everyone."

"How can I get out?" he asked.

"I don't know. But there must be a way."

Vulper growled. He had been listening all this time in a bored kind of way. "You try," he said, "and see what happens." I felt totally stuck.

Suddenly, Elvis turned his face back to the porthole. He looked excited – hopeful, even. "Big fish coming," he said quietly. "I can feel her."

"So is Silas," I whispered. "I can see him above us. He'll be here any second."

Elvis ignored me. He could sense something that I could not and he was getting dangerously excited. Those parts of him that were normally silvery-white were flushing rosy red. His golden bits were turning purple and his black bits shone like coal. Sheet lightning swept up and down his body and little golden sparks fizzed out of his mouth like sparklers on bonfire night. All of a sudden he made a noise like one hundred firecrackers going off. Flashes of white light shot out through the portholes lighting up the bottom of the loch with nightmare brilliance. Elvis's round black eye appeared in the middle off the porthole. His whole face was glowing scarlet and the rocket was beginning to sway.

"No Elvis! No!" I cried.

I turned and looked behind me. What Elvis had sensed, what had excited him so, was now just visible, looming through the darkness of the water. It was a huge, shadowy creature, something like a cross between a giant green lizard and a JCB. She had a long, lithe tail and a low-slung, knobbly body. Her legs were all elbows and claws, like crocodile legs, and her neck looked like a long green flume. Her head was small and neat and smooth-looking, with a long lizard-like nose, no chin, and golden eyes fringed with luscious eyelashes. Her skin was green and bumpy, like a gherkin.

At the same time as the creature began to emerge from the murky depths, Silas Stoatwarden appeared, plummeting towards us. He didn't see the creature at first; his eyes were glued to his precious rocket. He was in agony in case Elvis decided to blast off before he was ready. As Silas's flippers touched the bottom of the loch, the mighty creature stepped forward so that we could see her properly. She flicked her tongue out and

licked up a clump of water weed as though it was a bunch of carrots. When she swallowed I could see the weed going all the way down her flume. So could Silas Stoatwarden. He was staring up in horror at the huge green face that hung above him.

Slowly, so as not to arouse the creature's suspicions, Silas swung his harpoon gun around until it pointed straight at her. Beneath me, Vulper trembled with anticipation. Silas took a deep breath and squeezed the trigger. His harpoon hit the creature right in the middle of her chest. It bounced off. She glanced down, looped her flume in Silas's direction and stared at him with round gold eyes the size of rowing boats. Silas stared back, numb with surprise, still clutching his harpoon gun. Vulper sat down abruptly on the bottom of the loch. I found that my feet were touching the ground. I struggled free of my harness and scrambled off his back.

For several long seconds Silas and the creature stood nose-to-nose. Then she slowly opened her jaws. The last of the weed fell out, unchewed, as she picked Silas up and held him dangling delicately from between her big square teeth. She shook him gently, as a mother cat will shake a kitten, and flung him over her shoulder. He disappeared into the deep dark water of Loch Ness.

12 Safe Home

I didn't bother looking to see where Stoatface landed or even *if* he landed. I didn't give Vulper a second thought. I was watching Elvis and the creature. Love at first sight does happen – I know it does because I watched it happen, there, on the bottom of Loch Ness. Elvis gazed at Nessie from his small round porthole and she gazed back at him. Her golden eyes were overflowing with love. Gently, delicately, she leaned towards the rocket. Most carefully, so as not to injure Elvis, she bit right through the porthole. Next, she nibbled a hole in the fuel tank large enough for Elvis to glide out into the loch.

Then the two of them began to circle one another in the water. It was a strange dance of courtship, with Elvis firing off little bursts of sparks and lightning, while Nessie plodded slowly round in her own circle, undulating her long green neck. Every time their circles met, they smiled at one another, shyly. I began to feel that I was in the way.

I looked round to see where Vulper was, but he was long gone. "See you later, alligator," I told Elvis.

"In a while, crocodile," he chuckled.

I kicked off and headed for the surface, feeling happy and guilt-free. No more broken hearts for Elvis. He had found his true love after all. And no more ruler of the world for Silas Stoatwarden.

When I got up to the top I saw something that made me even happier. **SOFTIE** was parked on the heather right beside the loch! Tipperary had converted her back to a bus. I began to wave and holler, kicking out as best I could with my little diver's flippers. Hector heard me first. He took a flying leap into the loch and landed practically on top of me. "**Moses!**" he barked. joyfully. "**Moses! Yousafeyousafeyousafe!**"

Tipperary simply flew into the water, not even stopping to roll up her jeans. She scooped me up and held me close. "Holy Moly," she wept – but she was laughing at the same time. "We thought Silas Stoatwarden had got you and done something awful to you. We thought you'd gone for good, Moses. We were so frightened for you!"

"There, there, my girl," said Aunt Doris, who by now was standing on the shore, watching. "No need to smother the poor lad. Let's get him out of that nasty rubber suit and into a hot bath."

"But how did you find me, Tipperary?" I asked. "How did you know I'd be here?"

"We didn't, pet. Not for sure. But it's all thanks to Bess we found you – she picked up the scent of the submarine. She said it smelled fishy."

"That would be Vulper," I said.

Inside **SOFTIE** Aunt Doris was filling a large basin with warm water for my bath. Bess flew down from the top of the medicine cupboard and took up the story. "I could smell that cheesy smell all the way here," she said.

"Strongpong, strongpong!" Hector barked happily.

"We followed it," Bess continued, "and pretty soon we picked up Charley, floating in the water. He told us Silas had got you, and we just kept following. It wasn't hard – by then I was picking up whiffs of your nappy, Moses. We found the place where Silas landed and where he stuffed you and Elvis into the back of the lorry. We were dreadfully worried then – we thought you might suffocate."

"It took me a while to convert **SOFTIE** back into a bus," Tipperary explained. "We were so afraid that your trail would go cold, but Bess never lost it." All the chickens looked very proud when Tipperary said this. They crowded round Bess and made important clucking noises. Bess ruffled her feathers and flew back up to perch on top of the medicine cupboard.

Meanwhile, Tipperary peeled off my clothes. When she got to my nappy she gasped. So did

Aunt Doris. Everybody did, in fact. "Will you look at that dreadful nappy rash," Aunt Doris exclaimed. "That man ought to be run in. He ought to be charged with downright cruelty to babies. I don't know what ought to happen to a man like that, but it ought to be something nasty."

Tipperary lowered me gently into the basin of lovely warm water while Aunt Doris began to heat up milk for my bottle. It was only then that I remembered how ravenous I was. I began to cry, I couldn't help it, even though I was enjoying the warm, soothing water on my poor sore nappy rash. I didn't stop until I was wrapped in a big soft towel and cuddled on to Tipperary's lap with the teat of the bottle clamped between my lips. I sucked until the bottle was empty and cried for more. Tipperary gave me a whole big rusk to chew.

"Actually," I said, when I'd finished, "I think something nasty has happened to Stoatface already." That cheered everybody up. They felt even more cheerful when I told them about

Elvis and Nessie falling in love, and about Nessie throwing Silas over her shoulder like a punctured wellie. "I've never seen anyone look as scared as Silas did when Nessie picked him up and dangled him from her teeth," I said. "I'm certain he thought that she was going to eat him. I thought so, too – she's got teeth the size of tombstones. But she just shook him about a bit and chucked him over her shoulder. She didn't even look round to see where he landed, she went straight back to gazing into Elvis's eyes. I saw Silas go head over heels through the water. He hit the bottom and bounced a few metres and then I lost him. It's dark down there."

Charley Cool was wildly excited about Elvis and Nessie. "D'you think they'd give me an interview?" he asked. "For *News Round*? What a scoop – Nessie meets Elvis! It's better than *Blind Date*!"

"I think they'll want to be private for a while," I said. "Maybe you could ask them later."

Aunt Doris lifted me gently off Tipperary's lap. She asked Bess if any of the hens could spare an egg. As soon as one of the hens obliged, Aunt Doris cracked the egg and separated the yolk from the egg white. She whisked up the egg white with a fork and coated

my bottom with it. “Best thing in the world for nappy rash,” she told me. Then she put on my first clean nappy for days, snuggled me into a cosy babygrow and passed me back to Tipperary. I was home – home for now, anyway. My other home’s a long way off.

13 "HectorfightHectorbite!!"

Charley Cool cooked up a feast that night. There were toasted bread crumbs for the hens, herrings for Hector – he loves herrings – bean burgers and chips for Aunt Doris, Tipperary and Charley, and mashed rusks with custard for me. Hector and I had dandelion and burdock to drink – it goes up Hector's nose and makes him sneeze all over me but he likes it anyway. Aunt Doris and Tipperary and Charley had a bottle of wine.

After supper, Aunt Doris snoozed with her knitting in her lap. I leaned back against Hector's smooth shiny stomach and began to doze. Tipperary and Charley played scrabble for a while. Charley wrote *I love you* on the board – I could see the reflection in the window.

"Do you?" asked Tipperary.

"Yes, Yes, Yes!" Charley hollered, making Aunt Doris wake up and drop a whole row of stitches. "I've told you twice already!"

"Have you?" asked Tipperary. "I don't remember hearing you."

"You fell asleep both times before I got to the best bit."

"Sorry, Charley."

"It's OK. It's OK as long as you love me, too."

"I do," said Tipperary. "I really truly do."

After that everything went quiet.

Some time around midnight I was woken by a bloodcurdling howl. Hector leapt out of his basket, sending me tumbling, and stood with his fur bristling over his shoulders and his lips drawn back over his teeth, staring out of the window. There was no moon that night, you couldn't see a thing.

"W... what was that?" Tipperary asked in a trembling whisper. "It sounded like a w... werewolf, Charley."

"C... couldn't be a werewolf, angel pie," Charley answered. "They don't exist."

"Would you have said a giant electric eel from outer space existed, Charley?" Tipperary asked.

"Definitely not."

"Well then."

"She's got a point," Aunt Doris said. "There are more things in heaven and earth, Charley, than are dreamt of in your philosophy."

"How do you mean, Aunt Doris?" Charley asked.

"Never mind that," Tipperary whispered. "What I want to know is *who or what made that horrible noise*?"

"I know who made it," I said, sitting up in Hector's dog basket. "Vulper made it."

Hector bounced up and down on all four paws growling **"HectorfightHectorbiteHectorfightHectorbite!"** in his fiercest most ear-splitting growl. Before we could stop him he had pushed up the door latch with his nose and jumped outside. The howl came again, closer this time. It was lonely and lost and savage all at the same time and it made our hair stand on end. Charley tried to get Hector to come back inside **SOFTIE**, where he would be safe, but Hector wouldn't listen. Tipperary switched on **SOFTIE**'s headlights and there, caught in the beam, we saw a beastly sight. It was Vulper. His red eyes shone with an evil glint and green foam poured from between his triple rows of teeth.

"Stinker!" he growled.

"Stinkeryourself!" Hector growled back.

"Stupid Earth dog!" Vulper gargled. "Got no tail."

"Havehavehave!" Hector said, wagging his little stump. "Hectorgotsharpteethtoo!HectorfightHectorbite!"

Vulper stood still with a sneering look on his face; he was twice Hector's size and you could see he expected Hector to back off. But that's because he didn't know Hector. Hector isn't a backing-off sort of dog. He flew at Vulper and sank his teeth in deep.

Vulper was bigger and heavier than Hector. But Hector was fast on his feet and he had the advantage of surprise. As long as he held on to Vulper's neck he knew that Vulper couldn't twist his head round far enough to bite him. Vulper could kick and scratch, and he did both, but Hector hung on. They scuffled round and round one another, kicking up the heather. Vulper fell and Hector fell with him. They rolled right into the water but Hector still did not let go. Vulper got back on to his feet, dragging Hector up with him. His angry red eyes had a worried look. Hector hung on, snarling. Finally, Vulper began to make *OK I give in* signals. At first Hector didn't trust him – he thought it was a trick to get him to let go so Vulper could get his teeth into his throat. But soon it became clear to all of us that Vulper had had enough. Hector shook him like a rat and let go. Vulper scuttled out of the glare of the headlights into the moonless night.

We gave Hector three big cheers and a round of applause. We felt pretty proud of him – not many dogs would take on a Vulpeculan and win. Tipperary made him a medal for bravery and he wore it to bed in his dog basket. The fight had tired him out. He fell asleep at once and slept without so much as a twitch or a snuffle till morning.

We never did find out what became of Vulper. But Tipperary told me, once I was back home, that strange tales began to circulate around Loch Ness – stories of werewolves howling in the hills. Some folk said there was a new monster in the loch, a giant leopard-skin-coloured eel, but not many people believed that. Even so, those who lived close by the loch began to keep their cats indoors at night. They locked up carefully and sat beside their fires.

Nessie and Elvis were left pretty much in peace. A few TV stations sent reporters to search for the new monster but all they got was pictures of the loch.

As for Silas Stoatwarden, my guess is that he escaped somehow. I think he's still out there, waiting to cause more trouble.

The morning after Hector's battle was a sunny one. Light sparkled off the loch and shone on **SOFTIE**'s windows. Charley and Aunt Doris packed up while Tipperary cleaned the spark plugs. Then we were off again, searching for somewhere private for my pick-up. Tipperary knew just the spot. She drove us north to a mountain called Ben Hope. We parked **SOFTIE** and walked a long way up the mountain, leaving the other walkers and climbers far behind us. Tipperary and Charley took turns to carry me. Aunt Doris carried the picnic. Hector ran on ahead mostly. He was still wearing his medal and it glinted in the sunlight.

At last Tipperary said we had climbed high enough. She put me down in the heather and gave me my computer. I felt excited and sad at the same time – excited to be going home and sad to be leaving my friends. But I knew Dad would be checking his machine for messages, waiting to hear from me. I switched on my computer. [illegible] [illegible], I typed. [illegible] [illegible] [illegible] [illegible]. Which means "Eel sorted. Come and get me." I pressed the interplanetary key and sent the message on its way across the galaxy.

Tipperary blew her nose and Charley put his arm round her. Hector licked Aunt Doris on the face. Aunt Doris doesn't much like that but she knows that Hector means well. She wiped her face with her hankie and unwrapped the picnic. There was celery and salad and rice and peas and potato salad and biscuits and crisps and fruit cake and trifle with custard and cream on top. It was lovely. I got custard all over my face and Hector got cream behind his ears.

By and by, the sun began to sink towards the heather, turning the summit of Ben Hope soot black above us. Just as the sun went down, waves of colour filled the horizon. A far-off thrum made my heart beat faster. Then a familiar silver pod sank down out of the starry sky. It landed gently on the heather, the top opened and my father's voice floated out. "Well done, son," he said. "Well done."

SPACEBABY

by Henrietta Branford

WARNING!

The Earth is losing weight.
Everything's falling up
instead of down.
Gravity's gone wrong!

Can Spacebaby fix it before we all drop off the World? A computer game called Zucchini holds the key. Hector agrees to help. But Hector's no genius on computers, Hector's a dog.

Spacebaby and his friends race to save the Earth. But Silas Stoatwarden has other ideas... "I want the alien and I want him now!"

A **cosmic** story from the creator of the Smarties Prize winner *Dimanche Diller*.

"A delicious book, fast and funny and full of wonderful characters." *Guardian*

Collins

An Imprint of HarperCollins*Publishers*

www.fireandwater.com

DIMANCHE DILLER
by Henrietta Branford

When Dimanche is orphaned at the tender age of one, Chief Inspector Barry Bullpit advertises for any known relative to come forward. Unluckily for Dimanche, her real aunt does not see the message – but a bogus one does! So Dimanche, who is heir to an enormous fortune, is sent to live with the dreaded Valburger Vilemile, who tries to rid herself of Dimanche at every opportunity...

In 1995, *Dimanche Diller* won the Guardian Fiction Award, a prize awarded for the year's most exciting piece of children's fiction.

Collins
An Imprint of HarperCollins*Publishers*
www.fireandwater.com

DIMANCHE DILLER IN DANGER

by Henrietta Branford

Am safe and well but have been captured.
Try not to worry. Love, Dimanche.

Dimanche thought she had beaten her old enemy Valburga Vilemile, who's gone to prison. But locking Valburga up hasn't made her lose her evil cunning – her new plan to kidnap Dimanche and hold her to ransom is horribly successful...

A whizz-bang new adventure to follow the Smarties Prize-winning *Dimanche Diller*!

Collins

An Imprint of HarperCollins*Publishers*

www.fireandwater.com

DIMANCHE DILLER AT SEA

by Henrietta Branford

If there's one thing that's close to Dimanche's heart, it's her home. But proving it belongs to her is a problem, for somebody has stolen the Deed and Title. And there are strange happenings in the house...

"Dimanche Diller has established herself as a winning heroine." Julia Eccleshare, *Bookseller*

The latest adventure from this prize-winning author.

Collins

An Imprint of HarperCollins*Publishers*

www.fireandwater.com